# ROTTEN

Tyler H. Jolley

C.J. Xavier

# Tyler H. Jolley
# C.J. Xavier

*For my good friend Frank*

# Chapter 1

I had never seen a dead body before. Not like that. Up close and personal and not already crammed in a coffin at a funeral.

But that guy was dead. Not sleeping, mind you. Not unconscious.

He was a corpse with decaying flesh sliding off his rotten skull.

"Are you going to answer me or not?" a voice shouted from somewhere up the stone staircase. It belonged to my best friend, Jaylen Monroe. Jaylen had been waiting for me to give the all-clear, so he and the others could come down and join me—that was the deal.

"I'm good," I answered, steeling my nerves. "I'm at the bottom."

"Then why are you screaming like that?" Jaylen called out.

Panic filled me. Not from the corpse, but from my date and friends above hearing me scream. I hoped my high-pitched scream didn't bubble over so my date would notice. I had taken great care to never break that rule throughout my life, and I had been mostly successful until tonight. In all fairness, I had never expected to see a dead body. I couldn't believe I'd gotten myself into this. And over a lousy game of truth or dare, no less. I should have known Jaylen would dare me to do something *he* thought would impress my date.

"I didn't scream," I said. "I just slipped on something."

"Calvin, stop acting like a jerk!" Shelby Gibb's voice quivered with amazing volume. "If you're not back up here in five minutes, we're all leaving."

I smirked and rolled my eyes. Yeah right. How could she leave? I had the keys to my mom's Suburban, and I was her ride. I was all their rides, unless they wanted to start hoofing it several miles back into town.

"Seriously, this isn't funny." Shelby sounded like an obnoxious eight-year-old. I imagined her polishing her nose ring and checking to see if it still sparkled in the moonlight. That girl drove me nuts. I didn't see what Isaac saw in her. Why'd we bring them along?

"Do you want us to come down or what?" Jaylen's voice seemed closer now. He wasn't all the way down, probably still at the top of the staircase, but at least he had poked his head through the opening. "Shelby and Isaac are already heading for the gate."

"Fine!" I fired back. "They're going to miss out."

They never wanted to come in the first place. Shelby had called the whole trip to the mausoleum a bad idea. Maybe it wasn't the *best* idea, but we didn't have a ton of options in Jewkes, and there wasn't any movie worth watching at the Plex. I had hoped the creepiness of Hudson Cemetery would impress my friends, but I could sense I was striking out big time.

"Come on, man. Now Moira and Reyna are considering leaving as well. What do you want me to do?" Jaylen asked.

"Two minutes," I said. "Give me two minutes and then come down. I'm just looking at something."

To be honest, I wouldn't have minded if Jaylen had joined me. He would have appreciated this. The rest of my friends, on the other hand, would have pissed their pants. I hadn't told any of them about the body yet, because I wanted to experience everything for myself before anyone else joined in and things got muddled on who had discovered it first. Childish and immature maybe, but I didn't care. It wasn't every day you got to see a dead body.

Kneeling down, I pointed my flashlight toward the rotting remains of the man crushed beneath the rubble from what had to have been a roof collapse. The rocks had him pinned from the waist down, as well as most of his left side next to the wall. His right arm, rail thin and caked in dark, dried blood, rested atop more rubble. Fractured ribs poked out from his chest like gnarly barracuda teeth. The man's eyes were closed, sunken behind dark gray lids, and his face had shriveled like a putrid fish left on a dock in the summer's heat.

I could hear my heartbeat pounding in my temples.

"This can't be him," I whispered to myself. "Could it?" I instantly knew it couldn't be true the moment I uttered the words.

Everyone in Jewkes, Louisiana, knew about the Crenshaw Mausoleum. It was once open to the public as somewhat of a tourist attraction. Smack dab in the center of the mausoleum was an empty casket. No name markers. No dates. No one knew who it belonged to, but people would come from all over the state to see inside the empty stone coffin.

That was until twenty years ago, when Parry Hathspin,

a sixth-grader on a field trip with Griffin Elementary, fell through a crack in the floor and died. It turned out there was a whole other room beneath the mausoleum no one had ever known about. Of course, people didn't like it when someone died, especially a kid, and the mausoleum was deemed unsafe, and it was sealed up for good. But that kid was long gone, and dead people didn't age, which made it impossible for the corpse in the corner to be Parry Hathspin.

As I began brushing the dirt from my knees, I noticed something move out of the corner of my eye. I honed the flashlight in on the spot where I saw movement, and my breath caught in my throat.

The dead man's fingers were twitching.

Unable to blink, I watched as the corpse squirmed beneath the heavy load of rocks, mouth opening, struggling to breathe. His eyes flitted open. They were a dark yellow in color, but bloodshot, with obsidian pupils too large to be normal. I took a step backward toward the entrance, and his eyes widened, searching the room. After a few seconds of looking, he found what he was looking for.

Me.

We locked eyes, staring at each other for what had to be a solid minute, until he broke the silence with a raised hand, beckoning me to his side, finger joints popping with each motion. I shuddered. Icy chills ran up my back and into my ears. I sucked in a deep breath, but my breathing didn't slow.

"No way!" It was all I could think to say. My mouth had gone numb, and my brain had turned into a useless slab of muscle.

"Jaylen!" I shouted. "Get down here!"

My best friend didn't respond. I didn't have time to

create some rational thought process. Instead of listening to the voice of reason in my head, I rushed toward the man, knelt on the ground, and began tossing rocks off his lower body.

"Are you okay?" I asked.

The guy just moaned.

He was alive and I could help him.

The dude smelled horrible, like a bag of flaming dog crap. As I tossed rocks to the side, I began thinking about internal bleeding and how his organs should've been smashed to bits. Was I making a mistake by clearing the rubble? What if by doing so, I was just speeding up him dying?

The man tried lifting his chest from the floor and struggled a bit, unable to remove the load, but appeared determined to free himself.

"Don't do that," I said, my voice squeaking. "Just lie still while I go get help."

His old flannel shirt, the material all but rotted to pieces, tore away from the ground as he rose up, revealing a pool of dark muck beneath his back. His fingers tugged at my shirtsleeve, the nails impossibly long and his skin so transparent, I could see the brittle tendons and ligaments working beneath.

I had no idea how long he'd been down here, but something told me it hadn't been just a few days. How long, then? Weeks? Months? Without water, he would've died of thirst, not to mention the severe injuries sustained from the roof collapse. Those were ribs poking out through his chest! Small red worms pulled back into his open chest cavity as my light washed over them.

"Can't," the man whispered, opening his mouth, revealing black teeth and gray-colored gums.

The word caught me off guard. "What did you say?"

"C-can't," he repeated.

"What do you want me to do?" Where was Jaylen? I had told him two minutes. It was way past that, and I could really use his help.

The man dragged his swollen, cracked tongue across his lips. "Can't . . . reach."

Something heavy smacked the back of my head, and a flare of pain lit up behind my temples. My jaw fell slack, my ears rattled, and the room swirled before my eyes.

As I fell forward, collapsing in a heap, I felt the man's fingers digging at my throat.

And then darkness.

Everything black and empty.

My thoughts blank. No dreams. No sounds.

Nothing.

Except for thick nails piercing my skin.

# Chapter 2

For several minutes, I felt lost and dizzy. I wondered where I was. It didn't feel like my bed. Slowly, I sat up on the floor.

"You've got to be kidding me!" I spat.

I was still in the tomb beneath the mausoleum. But I must have crawled in my sleep, because I was no longer in the same room as before. Next to me, centered on the floor, was some strange stone with jagged edges. It stood more than six feet tall and was covered in weird drawings. One was definitely an eyeball with sharp teeth lining the eyelid. Another was some bird with human feet. And yet another was an image of a man with his hands plunged in the stomach of another figure lying on a slab.

The time on my watch read just after one, which meant I had been down in this part of the mausoleum for more than three hours. Why hadn't anyone come down to get me?

Then I remembered the man in the corner crushed beneath the rocks, and I leapt to my feet, facing the wall, my fists rising in defense. But he was gone. There was still a pile of stones where the ceiling had collapsed, but no one crushed beneath it.

"This is screwed up," I muttered.

I pawed at my neck and finally remembered what happened before I passed out.

Not wanting to wait around for any other weirdness to happen, I stumbled through the door and made my way back up the steps.

I staggered away from the mausoleum toward the rear entrance, hobbling over gravestones and calling out for my friends every few steps. Everyone had left. Maybe this was Jaylen's idea of some dumb joke.

"Another one of you kids? You can't be here!" It was Gorman Randolph, the cemetery caretaker, and he looked ticked, holding a flashlight in one hand and steadying his body with a cane in the other.

The old geezer charged after me, pointing the flashlight at me as if it were some light sword.

I ran, but probably didn't need to. I could've walked and gotten away just as easily from Gorman, but I didn't want to take any chances. After scaling the rear perimeter fence, I found Jaylen lying on the hood of my Suburban, completely asleep.

"Jaylen!" I startled him awake.

"It's about time, man!" he snapped, propping himself up on his elbows. "One a.m., bro. What were you doing?"

"What was I doing?" I asked. "Someone hit me over the head and knocked me out."

Swinging his legs around, Jaylen hopped down from the hood and rubbed his eyes. He raised an eyebrow suspiciously and smirked. "*Someone* hit you over the head?"

I sensed his sarcasm and dug my fingers beneath my

eyes in frustration. "No. Not someone. I didn't mean that. Something. Something hit me on the head. Like a rock."

I didn't feel ready to tell him about what I thought I saw down there. Maybe when things calmed down. "It must've dropped from the ceiling. I just barely woke up."

"No way," he laughed, not at all sympathetic to my obvious frustration.

"Yeah, and you were supposed to come down there, weren't you? That's what you said. It's been way longer than two minutes. And where's everyone else?"

Jaylen shrugged. "Gone home. Isaac called one of his loser friends and they came over and picked everyone up like two hours ago. I thought about going with them, figuring I'd get some action with Moira so the night wouldn't be a total failure, but then I couldn't just bail on you."

"What a great a friend," I muttered.

Jaylen started flipping the passenger-side door handle up and down. "Let's go, man. I've been sitting out here for like three hours."

Fishing out the key fob from my pocket, I pressed the automatic locks. Did Jaylen really think I should feel sorry for him? "Yeah, and I've been down beneath the ground, surrounded by caskets," I said. "I got chased by old Gorman and his flashlight just now."

"He chased us too," Jaylen reasoned. "That's why I couldn't come down. I called down a red alert to you that we were leaving. Didn't you hear me?"

I hadn't heard any red alert. Come to think of it, I couldn't remember much from earlier.

"We couldn't just hang out while Gorman swung his stick around trying to hit us."

Unsure of where to direct my anger, I climbed into

the car, waited for Jaylen to get in, and pulled away from the curb.

Ten minutes later, the Suburban sloped into Jaylen's driveway. I left it running and stared at my fingers gripping the steering wheel. They felt strange. Almost numb.

"You coming in?" Jaylen nodded toward the garage.

I shook my head. "I don't feel right." I touched my neck again. There were claw marks there. Or was I just imagining things? I shuddered. The thought of that corpse clawing at my jugular must've been in my imagination.

Jaylen flinched in surprise. "You're serious? I thought you were going to stay over. Are you ticked at me or something?"

"I'm not ticked." I mean, I had been and probably still was a bit, but Jaylen only did what anyone in his position would have done. And he had stayed behind to wait for me. No matter how hard I tried, though, I couldn't remove the image of the man from my thoughts. He *had* been down there. I knew he had. But where was he now?

"You sure?" Jaylen folded his arms, surprised by my decision.

"Yeah, I'm just going to go home and go to bed."

I didn't feel tired at all. Truthfully, I wanted to go home and think things through. Everything seemed hazy. Some sleep would do me good.

# Chapter 3

I stared at the glowing green numbers of my alarm clock with little fascination. When the time ticked to eight a.m., I finally decided there was no point trying to force sleep any longer. I'd had trouble falling asleep before, but this was different. I didn't even get undressed. For a good part of the night, I paced the room, feeling antsy, claustrophobic, and hungry.

Twenty minutes later, I sat at the dining room table, staring at a pile of scrambled eggs and three patties of sausage.

"What did you say?" I mumbled to my mom. She stood next to my chair, and I felt her eyes boring a hole in the side of my head as I tried sniffing my breakfast.

"I asked if you're feeling all right," she said. "You look sick, and you haven't touched your food."

I rolled my eyes, an action requiring much more effort than usual. They didn't actually roll, either. More like shifted slowly from side to side. I forked in a mouthful of eggs and swigged my juice.

"Why did you come home last night?" she asked,

finally sitting down at the table next to me. "I thought you were staying over at Jaylen's."

I responded with an unenthused shrug and stabbed a sausage patty with my fork. After examining the patty long enough to avoid making eye contact with my mom, I crammed it into my mouth. The eggs and sausage had no taste. I could've been chomping on a glob of Vaseline, and I wouldn't have recognized a difference.

"I think I'm getting a cold," I muttered through a mouthful of tasteless food.

My mom pressed the back of her hand against my forehead. "You don't feel warm. In fact, you feel a little clammy and cold."

I shrugged.

As if I needed her to tell me that. I didn't feel anything. I barely felt her hand. "You didn't do anything last night, did you?" she asked.

I glanced up from my plate, my eyes narrowing. "What do you mean?"

"You know what I mean. I like Jaylen, I really do." She sat with her arms crossed at her waist.

"But?" I pressed. She wasn't really going to start this conversation again, was she?

My mom plucked the carton of juice off the table. "No buts. I like him, but you have to be smart. I trust you to make smart decisions."

"I didn't drink, smoke, or snort anything last night, if that's what you're wondering," I groaned. "Just because he lives in Meadowbrook, it doesn't mean he deals drugs."

"That wasn't what I was wondering," she said, moving away from the table.

The rest of the Saturday passed by uneventfully. Well, except for the puking. I had barfed plenty of times before, but usually I had some sort of warning. I had been staring in the mirror, examining a premature zit poking up on my upper lip, when a yellow glob dropped from my mouth and splashed into the sink. Scrambled eggs, followed by slightly chewed sausage patties.

"What's wrong with . . ." I started to ask as another round of regurgitated eggs dribbled out. Bending over, I gripped the toilet seat, ready to ride out the sickness, but nothing more fell out.

I decided I needed to rest, plus napping was my favorite hobby. But sleep never came, and I was bored. My dad worked weekends, and my mom spent the day shopping with one of her girlfriends. I settled on occupying my time playing video games and staring longingly into the refrigerator for something we didn't have. I crammed an untoasted Pop-Tart in my mouth, just to quell the pangs. I didn't know what I wanted, but nothing in the kitchen appeased my hunger.

At three o'clock, I started throwing up again. Resting my elbows on the toilet seat, I caught my breath. I scratched my head with my fingers, and several strands of hair fluttered down like feathers. Alarmed, I dug into my scalp and came up with a handful of hair. Not just strands, but a whole clump!

"You've got to be kidding me!"

I had never seen that much hair fall out of my head before, and moved in front of the bathroom mirror for a closer look. Smacking the wall in frustration, I charged out of the bathroom. No doubt about it, I needed to see a doctor right away. Premature balding was not about to be in my near future.

A wave of relief swept over me as I heard the rumbling of the garage door. Bounding through the hallway, I hurtled over a pile of laundry, but I was too close to the stairs. As I tried to correct my mistake, I missed the first step and then the rest, as the bottom floor swiftly came up to greet me.

I heard a loud crash followed by a sickening snap. *Was that wood? Did I just break the handrail?* My dad was going to kill me. When my mom appeared in the room, she found me struggling to pull myself off the floor; my right forearm had snapped in two, and the bone was poking through the skin.

She dropped her bags and screamed.

# Chapter 4

"Bro, you stink," Jaylen said, pinching his nose and wafting away some invisible odor with his free hand. "Did you roll around in garbage or something?"

He held his baseball mitt in his lap, soaking it in a leather softening solution. I had always liked baseball as well, up until last year, when I didn't make the JV squad, but Jaylen obsessed over the sport. He never went anywhere without that glove.

I plopped down in the desk next to Jaylen in homeroom. If my ability to move around had slowed since the mausoleum, it had worsened with the addition of the new plaster cast on my arm. I kept ramming it into walls or getting it caught in doorways.

Dr. Oman, the orthopedic surgeon, had told my parents it was the cleanest break he had ever seen. No splintering, very little bleeding, and I was easily the calmest patient with a compound fracture. At first, he had assumed I was in shock, because my vital signs were all over the place. The doctor decided that it would be best to just set it in the office under conscious sedation. My dad wanted him to check me for drugs. Why was it always drugs with my parents?

I threw up nine more times over the weekend. First, it was the Otter Pops I ate while watching television Saturday evening. During a commercial break, up came the Otter Pops in my lap, still cold. On Sunday, I ate three bowls of cereal. Then, after I flushed the cereal, I vomited a ham sandwich for lunch, a couple sticks of string cheese, and leftover burgers for dinner. By Sunday afternoon, I could time the reappearance of my meals. Thirty minutes, almost to the second. Like clockwork.

I didn't sleep either. Not a wink. I figured my exhaustion would catch up eventually, and I'd crash on the couch, but that never happened.

"Maybe it's your cast." Jaylen's voice sounded nasally from the pinching.

"What?" I glanced down at the pasty white casing on my arm.

"Maybe your cast is stinking," he said. "You don't smell it?"

I stuck my nose next to it and inhaled, feeling the air travel through my nostrils, but not carrying even a faint hint of an odor.

"Seriously?" Jaylen was in a state of disbelief. "It's like worse than burning garbage. You smell like you have a dead raccoon in your backpack."

"Keep your voice down." I shot a quick glance around the room, making sure no one of importance might be listening to our conversation. Hot girls didn't date guys who disappeared for hours in a cemetery and stunk of garbage.

"You've made your point," I said. "We need to talk about something else. Something happened to me inside that mausoleum Friday night."

I had decided earlier that morning before sunrise, while I stared at the ceiling of my bedroom, unable to sleep, that I would tell Jaylen about the corpse in the tomb. I had to be careful, though. This was high school, not first grade, after all. If I didn't handle it tactfully, I might get labeled as a freak.

Jaylen raised an eyebrow, intrigued.

"Someone was down there in the tomb with me," I said.

Jaylen's eyes narrowed, then widened as he began to chuckle.

"I'm serious. I saw some man crushed beneath a ton of rocks. I thought he was dead, but he started moving. And when I tried to help him. I . . . I think he knocked me out."

"The dead guy?" Jaylen grinned.

"I said he wasn't dead," I snapped back.

"Where's he now?" He looked ready for a punch line. Unfortunately, I didn't have one to give him, but I wished I did.

"He wasn't there when I woke up," I said.

"So what you're saying is, some dead guy knocked you out and then got up and walked away?"

"Forget it." I sighed in annoyance. "I knew I shouldn't have told you."

Jaylen seemed ready to say something else, but instead heaved a groan as Shelby walked by the classroom, hand-in-hand with Isaac. She gave us a casual wave and continued down the hallway.

"I haven't slept since Thursday night," I continued. "And I puke up everything I eat." Since I had already spilled the weirdest bits to Jaylen, I figured I might as well go all out.

Someone had to understand my problem. My mom

called it a bug—just an internal reaction to breaking my arm. My dad vocally agreed with her, but deep down inside, I knew he figured it to be drugs. Surely, Jaylen, my best friend, would take a more empathetic angle. Maybe even offer me some sound advice. I nervously scratched my chin even though it didn't itch.

After several seconds of contemplation, Jaylen sighed. "Do you think Shelby would care if I punched that idiot in the head?"

"I'm talking for real here," I said, agitation rising in my voice.

Jaylen's eyes shifted from the doorway back to me. "You're right. I should hit Shelby instead. Knock some sense into that hollow brain of hers."

As I ran my fingers through my hair, I flinched when I felt the all-too-familiar tangle of strands unhitching from their follicles. My hair was still falling out, one thick clump at a time. Discreetly keeping my eyes on Jaylen as he sat watching the doorway and, no doubt, hoping Shelby would appear and leap into his arms, I lowered my hand to my side and dropped the tangle of hairs to the ground.

"Are you done drooling over Shelby yet?" I asked.

Jaylen blinked. "I'm not drooling, am I?" He grinned, but only fleetingly, and then his face grew serious. "Check this dude out." He flicked his chin toward the hallway and I followed his gaze out the door.

Our homeroom stood at the cross of a T intersection of the sophomore wing, with classrooms stretching down either direction and a straight shot to the gymnasium at the far end of the building.

"What's wrong with him?" I asked, noticing a man standing at the end of the hallway.

A lot of people, parents or visitors, entered in through

the gymnasium doors and eventually wandered over to the offices to check in.

"He just keeps staring at me," Jaylen said.

For some reason, I knew the man wasn't staring at Jaylen, and his gaze caused my stomach to churn. I felt like I had seen him before. It was the type of recognition one would have for someone they had bumped into at a family reunion.

"Quit staring at me," Jaylen hissed through gritted teeth. He had a problem with people staring at him unless they were girls. So basically, he always had a problem.

"What are you staring at?" he called out more forcefully.

After a moment's pause, the man slid sideways into the gymnasium and disappeared.

The dull thudding of my heartbeat pounded in my ears. I needed to eat. It was the only thing that mattered at the moment, but nothing sounded good to me. I eyeballed Jaylen's half-eaten bag of potato chips, tipped sideways on his desktop, and grabbed for them. As I devoured the chips, gobbling up even the crumbs like a vacuum, Jaylen gawked at me in disbelief.

"Those were mine!" He laughed, his expression still baffled.

I ignored Jaylen, my eyes darting around the room in desperation. "I need to eat . . ." I gasped, my words escaping in short breaths.

"Settle down, bro."

Jaylen reached over to steady me, but my hand suddenly shot out, swatting the baseball glove off his lap and raking a deep, bloody groove across his leg with my fingernails. Jaylen gasped, pressing his hand to the wound, his eyes contorting with a mixture of pain and surprise.

My mouth went slack. "I'm sorry, man," I said, staring down at my hand, taking note of Jaylen's dark skin beneath my fingertips. "I didn't mean for that to happen."

Jaylen swore and pushed himself up from his desk. "What's the matter with you?" He shoved my shoulder, and I fell back in my chair.

The various conversations of my classmates stopped abruptly, and I sensed several pairs of eyes watching us, waiting to see if our argument would go any further. A couple of them, Maurice Tillman and Greg Hollister, Jaylen's teammates on the baseball team, stood up on their chairs in the back of the room, peering over the class as Jaylen balled his hands into fists.

"Jaylen, don't," I begged. "It was an accident. I swear."

I desperately scanned the classroom, hoping to see some sort of authority figure who could break up the fight before it escalated, but Mr. Griggs was never present during homeroom. He always spent the half hour filling his gigantic coffee mug down in the lounge. Would Jaylen punch me? Would we actually fight?

"Do it!" Maurice shouted from the back of the room. His laugh became a dentist's drill in my ears. "Smash him!"

I turned toward Maurice and felt my rage returning. I didn't want to hurt Jaylen, but Maurice . . . that was a different story. A grotesque image of his head appeared in my mind: cracked open on the ground, with me hovering over the carnage. Blood seeping around his head . . . brains spilling out like the innards of a smashed pumpkin.

Jaylen snapped me back into reality, but instead of hauling off, he peered over his shoulder at the two morons and stooped down to retrieve his baseball mitt from the ground.

"Calm down, ladies," Jaylen said to his teammates,

easing the tension with a chuckle. "No one's getting smashed today."

I breathed a sigh of relief. Jaylen and I had been best friends for a few years now, but I had mistakenly challenged his bravado in front of the whole class. You just didn't do that sort of thing in high school. My thoughts again returned to my fingers and the tufts of skin poking out beneath the nails. Jaylen's skin. How could I have done that?

The bell for first period rang and everyone began shuffling out of their desks.

"Seriously, man, I'm sorry," I said. "I was just mad, you know? Because you weren't listening."

"No, I heard you." Jaylen stood and pounded his fist into the mitt. "You were attacked by a dead guy and now you're barfing up everything and not sleeping. Maybe you're pregnant. Stop being a wuss." He shouldered his backpack and headed for the door. "I'll catch you later."

# Chapter 5

I sat in bed later that night, wearing a T-shirt and boxers, and as usual, wide-awake and starving. As I shifted under the covers, a strange feeling came over me.

Someone was watching the house. I didn't know how I knew it, but as I crossed the room and parted the drapes, I discovered a stranger standing in the driveway and recognized him almost at once. He still wore the same clothing from earlier, when Jaylen had noticed him in the hallway. It was the visitor at the high school. The man Jaylen thought was gawking at him, but it had been at me all along.

What did he want? I felt curious and hungry—oh so hungry—and the urge overtook me. Suddenly, I lunged toward the window, smacking it with my forehead and cracking the glass. I felt no pain, and I didn't even care if the sound had woken my parents. My vision blurred for a moment, and then I found myself standing next to the man out in the driveway, with no memory of having left my house.

"You . . ." I started to say, but the man's finger silenced me.

It was then I noticed the brown paper sack clutched in his hand and went for it, but he withdrew a step, pulling the bag out of reach.

"Not here," he whispered, nodding toward the end of the road. "Walk with me a bit and I'll let you have a bite." He shook the sack and I nodded vigorously.

We walked for a long time, all the while my eyes staying glued to the brown package. I had no idea where he was taking me, which should have freaked me out, but I didn't care. He could've taken me anywhere. Locked me in some basement. Only the contents of that paper sack mattered now.

When we finally stopped, I took a moment to look around and saw that we were somewhere in the city. A narrow alleyway splintered off from a main strip of road, with cars sleeping next to metered parking. I noticed graffiti on the walls and garbage littering the sidewalk, and judging by the lack of activity, most of the businesses had closed for the night. I glanced toward the flickering streetlamp across the road from the alley as a couple of cars sped past, and a neon sign on one of the buildings announced our location: the Cobalt, a bar almost seven miles from my home that doubled as a karaoke lounge on the weekends and stayed open late. Jaylen's dad was a regular there.

"Who are you?" I asked, wondering why I had allowed some stranger to lure me away from the safety of my house.

The man raised his finger and placed the sack in front of him on the ground. He opened it, his hand vanishing into the paper and returning, holding a glob of something gray and glistening. His nostrils flared as he passed the meat into my outstretched hands, and an instant jolt of electricity hit my mouth.

Never in my life had I tasted anything so divine. I wanted to savor every bite as my teeth ground the sinewy substance, but due to my hunger, I couldn't resist gobbling it down in three massive swallows. Another glob passed to my hands with the same result. Down and gone in seconds. The man ate as well, and we shared our meal in relative silence, though I could hear myself breathing erratically, like a dog begging for table scraps.

I devoured ten pieces and was left licking my fingers. Finally, I felt full, and somehow, I knew I wouldn't vomit up this meal.

"Can we talk now?" I asked, licking my lips.

The man tossed the sack into the dumpster and pulled a handkerchief from his pocket, wiping the stickiness from his fingers.

"My name's Belmont," he said, offering me the handkerchief, which I reluctantly accepted. It was wet and covered in slime, but it was better than wiping my hands on my . . .

"What the?" I stared down at my T-shirt and boxers. "Where are my clothes?"

Belmont's eyes gave me a quick appraisal. "Don't ask me. That's what you chose to wear."

Why didn't I think to change into something a little more appropriate for a midnight rendezvous in some dark alley? I was miles from my home and standing in my underwear.

"Never mind that, why did you bring me here? Are you some kind of stalker? And what was that stuff we just ate?" I instinctively ran my fingers through my hair and winced as I felt the give of a clump detaching from my scalp.

"You'll need to see to that first." Belmont nodded to the blond hairs in my fingers. "That's an easy fix."

"My hair?" I looked up at him, startled.

"Unless it's now all the rage to go bald in high school."

"I'm not going bald," I scoffed. "My mom says I need more vitamin E. Tell me why I'm here."

"Calvin, I brought you here"—Belmont motioned with his hands to the walls of the alley—"because we needed privacy and seclusion."

"So you picked an alley across from the Cobalt? There's a park three blocks from my house, still practically in my neighborhood. We could've had seclusion there. And why do we need privacy in the first place?"

"You will need time to think after tonight, and a long walk will do you good. You could try suturing." Belmont pulled his own hair back by the part. "It's very lifelike and more permanent." The strands of black hair appeared natural at first, but upon closer examination, I could see where each clump had been affixed permanently to the scalp. "Expensive, but I'm sure I could arrange for an appointment. I know someone who handles these situations delicately."

"Forget my hair!" I demanded. I needed to go home. I had school in the morning, and if my parents happened to wake up and check in on me, they'd call the cops.

Belmont chuckled. "Relax. I'm here because I know what's happening to you."

"What is happening to me?"

"You've lost feeling in most of your senses, and the others are dimming by the day. You're losing your hair, you can't stomach normal food or drink, you're starting to smell, and your skin is beginning to fester. Have I missed anything?"

Belmont had just rattled off my symptoms like a printed grocery list.

"Are you some kind of doctor?" I asked.

"You have contracted a rare strain of Lich Somnambulus."

I blinked in confusion. "And what is that?"

"Your body has been reanimated."

"Like a cartoon?" I should have the urge to leave . . . I couldn't explain why I felt compelled to listen.

Belmont appeared to contemplate his next choice of words. "Something happened to you recently to cause this. Do you remember what it was?"

I sniffed and licked my lips again, still faintly catching the flavor of my earlier meal. I wanted another bite, but not because I was starving anymore. On the contrary, I could feel my stomach distending, like one of those malnourished children in a developing country. I just wanted to taste it again.

"Calvin?" Belmont pressed, and I snapped back from my daydream.

"Yeah, I went into the Crenshaw Mausoleum on Friday night and hit my head and then all this started." I wished Jaylen and I had gone to a movie and played video games instead. It would have been better than spending the whole weekend puking. Of course, I didn't say any of that to Belmont.

"You bumped your head?" he probed. "Nothing else? You don't recall seeing or feeling something?"

I shifted my weight uncomfortably. "Yeah, I saw something else. There was a man trapped under the rocks. I tried helping him, but then . . . I guess he was crazy and he attacked me. I got knocked out, and when I woke up, he was gone."

I looked over Belmont's shoulder as a car passed. It

was time for me to leave. If this freak was all out of food, I saw no point in carrying on our discussion.

"Look, thanks for the grub, but I gotta go."

"What else did you see?" Belmont asked, leaning forward.

"I saw some weird stone with numbers all over it." Had they been numbers? No. Not numbers or words, more like symbols, but why would he care about that?

Belmont smiled. "It's called a Lich Stone. A pathway marker."

"Leech stone," I repeated. "That's like the second time you've used that word. I don't know what it means."

The neon sign of the Cobalt flickered off as two men stumbled out the entryway and nearly toppled over the first step. Unless the Cobalt closed early on Mondays, it meant the time was already close to four a.m. How long would it take to get home? Seven miles was no easy stroll. I felt uncomfortable under Belmont's gaze. I couldn't help noticing his teeth. They were way too white. Like my grandmother's dentures. Did he have false teeth? He couldn't be that old, could he? I guessed maybe in his early forties.

"Your hair fell out, didn't it?" I asked. "I'm guessing your teeth did as well."

Belmont nodded. "Hair and teeth are the first to rot. That's your warning. The next changes won't be so subtle. Fortunately, you are not alone. There are others plagued with this condition. Some I know very well."

"Leech, um, soma," I tried repeating the term Belmont had mentioned earlier.

"Somnambulus," he enunciated. "The translation means a form of sleepwalking."

"Right there you lost me," I said. "I haven't slept for even a second since this thing happened. Every night, I just sit in bed and wait for the morning, so I can get up and move around and not wake my parents. I don't sleepwalk, because I don't sleep. I just walk."

Belmont sighed. "You just don't understand the nature of this condition."

"Then tell me!" I snapped, feeling my temper heating up. "I don't have all night."

"Lich comes from a German translation," Belmont began.

I turned to leave; I didn't have time for this.

"It means corpse."

I turned on my heel. "Corpse?" I blurted out.

"Lich Somnambulus means a sleepwalking corpse." Belmont tilted his head to the side, offering me a saddened look. "Or, if you'd prefer . . . a zombie."

The word hit me square in the jaw, and I stumbled backward, my back colliding with the dumpster. Belmont placed his hands on my shoulders to steady me. I wanted out of the alley and to be as far away from him as possible.

"The man you saw in the mausoleum attacked you," Belmont said. "He was a zombie, and unfortunately, you died Friday night."

"You're nuts. No . . . you're wrong . . . I . . ." I stammered.

Ignoring my interruption, Belmont continued. "He transferred his disease into your bloodstream, which caused your body to change, and somehow you came back. I can't explain the reason why, but now you are placed in an interesting situation."

"I'm not dead," I said, the words escaping with mocking laughter as I pulled away from him. "You think I'm dead?"

Despite the absurdity of his suggestion, there seemed

to be a nagging truth to it. My hair, my skin, my eyes. Something unnatural had started happening to them . . . to me.

"I'm not here to frighten you. On the contrary, I can help," Belmont said. "The good news is there are practices and steps you can take to fit back into society. A hundred years ago, you could forget about all that. This curse ended any chance of adaptation. But due to medical advances, life can go on for us as zombies."

There was that word again.

It was almost too humorous to handle. I had seen dozens of movies with zombies ambling around burning cities, attacking every human.

Belmont continued to talk, but I wasn't listening anymore. Instead, I removed my cast. The plaster wrap tore off in two long, continuous strips. I felt along my forearm, finding where the break had ruptured the skin, and inserted my finger, shuddering at the feeling of dense bone. It was like touching a solid piece of wood. Dry and maybe cold. I couldn't feel temperature anymore, but I sensed the bone lacked the normal amount of heat. I was probably grazing over severed nerve endings, my fingers passing through broken arteries and veins, but I felt no painful sensation.

"Calvin?" Belmont's voice cut through my trance. "Have you been listening?"

I glanced toward the other end of the alley, wondering if it emptied into a populated neighborhood. Did it have access to a main road? I didn't care. I needed to get as far away from Belmont as possible. Pushing off from the dumpster, I made my way around a cardboard box packed full of old newspapers.

Belmont hurried after me. "We're not finished here. There's more I need to explain."

"No, we're done." I continued walking.

"You have needs now. Needs I can provide for. You can carry on a normal existence, but you don't have much time."

"Oh, you want to help me? I have *needs*? That sounds like a great way to end up on one of my mom's murder shows."

"You don't understand—"

"Shut up!" I snapped. "Just shut up! And if you come around my neighborhood or to my school anymore, I'm going to call the cops." Upon my outburst, Belmont stopped following me.

Once out of the alley, I felt relief when I recognized the road. Canterbury Avenue wound around an industrial area of town, but it would be empty at this hour, and I could walk in silence. I needed time alone, time to distance myself from one of the strangest nights of my life. Time to think.

And figure out why there wasn't blood inside my broken arm.

# Chapter 6

After our little late-night snack in the alley, I made it through the next day of school mostly unscathed. I didn't bother with breakfast or lunch, knowing I wouldn't have too many opportunities to duck out of class to go vomit it back up.

During World History, I made my peace with Jaylen.

"Look, dude, I'm sorry," I whispered during some boring film about the *Lusitania*.

Jaylen shrugged. "Yeah, I know you're sorry. And guess what? You still stink."

I looked at my armpits, and though I smelled nothing, I knew he was right. My mother had purchased two new sticks of deodorant and left them by the bathroom sink with a bottle of aftershave that morning. I didn't shave too often, which meant she was suggesting I just needed to wear some regardless.

"Any more attacks from dead guys?"

If only he knew the extent of it.

I noticed a large bandage taped to Jaylen's leg where I had scratched him yesterday.

"How's the leg?" I asked.

Jaylen glanced down for a second and brushed it off. "It's fine."

"Come on, man. Do you want to scratch me back? I'll let you sock me right in the nose, if you'll just forgive me."

The slide on the projector screen flashed to a sinking ship, which captured our attention for a few moments before it switched to something else. I debated telling Jaylen about what happened last night. Would he try to help me, or would he make fun of me some more? Then I thought about showing him the bald spot smack dab in the back of my head. Yeah, I had one that was growing bigger by the minute. I looked like a forty-year-old with a bad comb-over. In the end, I settled on inviting him over to play video games after school.

Jaylen considered my offer. "We'll see," he said.

***

After school, Jaylen texted to let me know he was coming over. The things I did to secure my friendship. For the next two hours, we binged on soda and nachos and beef jerky. Some would call it self-mutilation. Every thirty minutes, I had to nonchalantly weave my way to the bathroom to destroy the toilet, but I did it for Jaylen. I needed my best friend back, and I knew junk food and mindless video games would deliver. We even played *War of the Dead*, a first-person shooter game where you slaughtered thousands of zombies in a village in Central America. Every time a head exploded or brains splattered on the screen, I inwardly shivered. It was hitting too close to home.

In the end, Jaylen and I were square. We even shared a good laugh over our little encounter in homeroom.

After that, we just lounged on the couch, finishing off the remains of the food.

Jaylen released a deafening belch. "I can't believe you broke your arm," he said. "Baseball is out for you now."

"I know, it's stupid, but do you want to see something really weird?" I asked.

He shrugged as I undid the makeshift bandage I had reapplied before school that morning. It was a bold move, but I wanted him to see the injury. Maybe then he'd be willing to hear me out about my other problems.

Jaylen took one look at the hole in my arm and his face turned a nasty shade of gray. "I'm gonna be sick. That smells like . . . bad cheese. Wrap it back up!" he demanded.

I ignored his plea and instead jabbed my finger into the wound.

Jaylen dry heaved. "What's the matter with you? You don't feel that?"

"Nope." I shook my head and extended my arm toward him for a closer look.

"I will throw up all over your couch!" Jaylen said in a raised voice.

"What do you think I've been doing in the bathroom all evening long?" I asked.

Despite his continual retching, Jaylen kept his eyes glued to my arm. "You were throwing up?"

I nodded.

"You're sick?" He scooted away from me on the couch.

After a few more seconds, I finally surrendered to Jaylen's pleading and covered my arm with the bandage. "That's not the only problem. Look at this." I tugged gently on my hair and easily pulled out a hundred strands.

This caused an eruption of laughter as color returned to Jaylen's cheeks. "You're losing your hair too?"

I laughed as well, but there was nothing behind it. "It's not funny," I said. "Something's wrong with me."

"There's nothing wrong with being bald." Jaylen chuckled, dragging his hand across his completely shaved head. "I am, and it makes the girls go crazy."

"Yeah, but yours is a conscious choice," I said. "There's nothing I can do to stop this."

For the first time in as long as I could remember, Jaylen turned serious. "You need to go to the hospital. All joking aside. Maybe you caught cancer."

"You can't catch cancer," I said, tugging on the tape and fastening it across the bandage.

"You know what I mean. Hair falling out. Arm looking all gangrenous."

I smirked. "Gangrenous?"

"It's a word," Jaylen said. "You don't play around with something like this."

He might be right. A hospital visit definitely sounded like a reasonable option, but I wasn't finished with my grand reveal yet.

"Do you remember that guy from school the other day?" I asked.

Even though the bandage had it completely covered, Jaylen still hadn't looked up from my arm. "What guy?"

"The one staring at me in homeroom."

Jaylen's eyebrows rose slightly. "The weird pervert?"

"That's the one," I said. "He visited me last night."

Jaylen opened his mouth, but said nothing.

"I followed him into an alley across from the Cobalt, and we ate food together." That sentence had to be the most ridiculous-sounding words I had ever spoken. And there I sat, sharing it with Jaylen Monroe. "He said I had some sort of disease, like a sleepwalking-type disease, but he said he could help me."

"Let me get this straight." Jaylen's eyebrows pinched together. "You followed some guy—some *old* guy—to the Cobalt in the middle of the night?"

I knew it. I had made a bad mistake telling Jaylen, and I needed a way out of it. I held my serious look for just a moment more, and then erupted with laughter. Jaylen stared a moment longer and then cracked. We laughed for several minutes. His eyes watered. I spilled nacho cheese dip on the carpet, and then he punched my chest.

"I almost thought you were serious," he said, wiping his nose with the back of his hand. "I thought I was gonna have to tell your parents or something."

"Yeah, good one, huh?" I replied.

Maybe I had dodged a bullet. We might be best friends, but secrets told to Jaylen had a way of spreading to every sophomore's ears. I would just forget about it. Forget everything I had told him. Do whatever it took to get back to normal.

But later that night, long after Jaylen had gone home and my parents were snoring in their bedroom, I once again snuck out of the house and went looking for Belmont.

# Chapter 7

Belmont knew a whole lot about me, and he had the answers. More importantly, I hoped he had that paper bag of food. Before the last couple of nights, I had never tried sneaking out, but now I wished I had. It was way too easy. I just walked right out the door and my parents never stirred. All this time, I could've gone out and done . . . what? Hung out with Jaylen? We didn't have girlfriends, and there was no way we could pass as adults to go clubbing. I guess I wasn't really missing out, but still. So easy.

I considered taking the Suburban, but couldn't think of a way I'd be able to roll out of the garage and down the driveway without creating a ton of noise. Instead, I snagged my bike and took off down the darkened streets in search of Belmont.

I didn't have to go far.

The strange man sat on a bench in the park a few blocks from my house.

"Very impressive," he said, rising from the bench as I applied the brakes and dismounted.

"What's impressive?" I asked. "The fact that I found you?"

Belmont clucked his tongue. "No, I had no doubt you'd find me. But I was impressed with your ability to ride so smoothly. You have surprising resilience to the infection."

I looked down at the bike and jabbed a finger in my ear. "Look, I don't really want to talk to you, but I was hoping you brought that sack lunch of yours."

There was no point in beating around the bush. I didn't like Belmont. Why the creep had a fascination with me was hard to understand. Maybe we both suffered from similar conditions, but should that have suddenly made us best friends? I had a mild form of acid reflux, but that didn't mean I went looking for friends down the antacid aisle at Walmart. I didn't look into Belmont's eyes, but I felt certain they were gleaming at me. He knew he had what I needed, which probably made his day.

"You're hungry," he stated.

As if that came as some big surprise. Did he think I itched for more stimulating conversation on his psychopathic ideas about zombies?

"Yeah, I'm hungry." I glanced down at the park bench, searching for his grab bag of delights.

Belmont frowned. "I didn't bring anything with me."

My stomach lurched and my arms fell dejectedly at my sides. How could he not have anything? My hunger was going to drive me insane.

"But not to worry," he added quickly, as if sensing my inevitable explosion. "If you'd like, I can take you to a place to get more. You'll want to feed a lot at the beginning. But then the hunger subsides, and eating every few days will do."

I had no idea what he was talking about. All that mattered was I was famished, and he didn't have anything for me to eat.

If I left Belmont and vowed again never to return, how long would I last? A few hours? Maybe a day? If he had access to more food, I needed it to survive—plain and simple. But if I went with him, it might create a pattern of late-night meetings. And how would I explain that to my parents? Sixteen-year-olds in Jewkes generally didn't have much of a nightlife.

"Can we make it quick?" I asked.

"I can't promise that," he admitted. "What we're about to do is not exactly legal, and we run the risk of getting caught. It would be impossible for me to guarantee any of this will be done quickly."

"Not legal?" I took a step back. "Aren't we just going to some all-night store where you can buy that meat?"

"No store, unfortunately," he said. "But there's no other way to get what we need."

After another moment's pause, I nodded in agreement. What choice did I have?

For the second night that week, I found myself following the strange man, walking in almost complete silence. I left my bike by the park bench, and though he couldn't promise a quick jaunt to the grocery store for grub, Belmont assured me we'd be back to retrieve it before sunrise.

We walked for a few miles with him in front, I a couple steps behind, until I once again recognized the familiar glow of the Cobalt's neon lights. Belmont gestured toward the alleyway, but this time we didn't pause by the dumpsters. Instead, we continued, stopping at an old door, almost hidden in the alley beside a frosted window with red lettering etched into the glass. I gave the sign a fleeting glance, but years of neglect had made the words illegible.

Bending down, Belmont pushed aside a mud-covered boot and picked up the key hiding beneath it. After fidgeting with the knob, he unlocked the door. Through barely a sliver of an opening, Belmont stared in, breathing quietly. I knew not to disrupt him on the off chance someone dangerous might be on the other side of the door. After all, he said it wouldn't be legal. It certainly didn't feel on the up and up.

Satisfied, Belmont opened the door wider, stepped through, and turned back to me.

"Wait here," he instructed.

I didn't object, and after a couple of minutes, he returned, allowing me to enter. Once inside, Belmont clicked on a flashlight he had retrieved from somewhere in the building. Not sure of what to expect, I stumbled down three short steps and nearly knocked over a trash can. I felt my femur bend, but fortunately nothing broke with this fall. After apologizing in a whisper, I quickly assessed that we were in some sort of mudroom. A shoe rack with four or five pairs of boots and slippers rested by the small flight of steps. A coat hanger with a windbreaker and a fleece jacket hung to the area above the rack, and on both sides of the room, cabinets crowded the walls. A couple of the doors stood ajar, but their contents weren't visible by flashlight.

"Don't touch anything," Belmont said. "I've been fortunate enough to make some unique acquaintances who have graciously allowed me access to their property. I don't want to ruin a good thing."

"You know the person who lives here?" I asked.

"Works here," Belmont corrected. "Yes, I know them very well."

"What do they do besides hawking food on the black market?"

"They own a small comic book store out on the other side of the building."

"Comics?"

"Yes, but their oldest son works at the morgue."

"Okay, don't think I really needed that information, did I?" I asked.

Belmont sighed. "Do you want to continue this conversation, or would you rather eat?"

"Eat." I felt anxious. Unsettled. And I half-expected some burly dude covered in prison tattoos to suddenly appear in the darkened room, ready to make me his girlfriend.

"You don't need to know anything else. You won't meet them," Belmont assured me. "They've already left. That's how this works."

"Then what's the big deal? I mean, if you know them and they let you use this place, we're not exactly breaking any laws, are we?" Kneeling, I opened one of the cabinets for a better look. Inside, I found a few cleaning supplies, but nothing I wanted to eat.

Belmont pressed the flashlight against my shoulder. "I said don't touch anything." His voice was firm. "And we haven't broken any laws *yet*. That's the key word. It's what we're about to do."

I stood and seriously considered the exit. Now was as good a time as any to be on my merry way. I wasn't a criminal, and I didn't want to lead that sort of life. Surely, there were other ways to stay fed with my condition.

"Calvin, listen to me very carefully. When we go into the next room, you're not going to like what you see. It may cause you to want to yell out. You mustn't do that," Belmont instructed. "Stay calm, take deep breaths, and focus your mind on something else. This will all be very clear to you shortly."

"I don't think I want to do this after all," I said, firmly grasping the handrail.

"Suit yourself." Belmont moved away from the stairs toward another door. Glancing back at me, almost tauntingly, he opened the door wide enough for me to see through. Resting slightly off-center in the next room, perched upon what looked like an operating table, was a body.

# Chapter 8

I should have felt the urge to run.

I wanted to believe the man on the slab was only sleeping. That, after a long day at work and finding no better place to rest, he had chosen to climb up on a table covered in a white sheet and take a nap. And that little cardboard note dangling off his foot? That wasn't a toe tag. No, that was just the price label from off his sneakers.

But make no mistake about it, that man was stone dead.

And I did want to run . . . *toward* the body.

I had no way of knowing how long it had been since his passing. Actually, that was kind of a stupid thing to say. Unless you were some sort of expert, no one should know how long someone had been dead just by looking at him. I couldn't smell him because I couldn't smell anything anyway, but he didn't look in the process of decomposing like the guy in the mausoleum. So I guessed it had happened maybe a couple of nights before. His closed eyes rested sunken back behind the lids. His skin had started to turn blue, and his body, which, by the way, was completely naked, bulged from bloating. Other than that, he seemed to be in decent shape, considering he was a corpse.

The worst part about it? I knew him.

Not personally, mind you. I had never talked to the man before, but I had seen him around. Jewkes wasn't a big place. I didn't know his name, but I thought he might have worked at a hardware store in town.

A jolt of electricity coursed through me. It should've been fear or alarm, or jaw-dropping shock, but instead, the hunger pangs struck me like lightning. Instantly, I was drawn into the room.

As I approached the dead man, I shoved my hands into my pockets, unsure of what I'd do to this man if I didn't exhibit *some* self-control.

"Do you want to know how he died?" Belmont's hands rested on the dead man's shoulders. The skin beneath his fingers bunched up ever so slightly, as if the man's body were made of clay. I didn't respond. Couldn't respond. I just stared at the corpse. Two dead bodies in less than a week. This was becoming an odd habit of mine.

"Heart attack," Belmont said. "He was forty-six years old, with apparent high cholesterol. It's not uncommon for his age, particularly when it runs in his family." Belmont's head tilted to one side as he continued. "Woke up two nights ago in bed, went for a glass of water in the kitchen . . ." He sucked back on his teeth. "His wife found him the next morning sprawled out on the linoleum. Shame."

I finally pulled my attention away from the man's eye sockets, though I swore one of the lids threatened to fly open.

Belmont laughed suddenly. Alarmed, I asked, "Why

are you laughing? No, never mind that. Why is he *here*?"
I immediately thought of my own parents and how tragic
it would be to happen upon one of them lying dead in my
kitchen. This wasn't funny at all.

Belmont clamped his hand over his mouth, stifling
the laugh, and forced away his obnoxious grin. "You're
right. It's not funny. It's horrible. This man had a family
and a good life, and now it has ended."

"I don't get you."

"One day you will. Maybe not right away. I can still
remember the way I felt when it was my first." Belmont
stroked his chin. "That was so many years ago, but I can
still remember the apprehension of it all. When I saw the
look in your eyes, I saw myself, and I just couldn't help
but laugh."

"Whatever, man. Where's the food? I'm all touched
you wanted to show me this dead guy. Truly. Maybe he's
your relative, or I'm sure you thought I'd appreciate this,
and so it means a lot." I crossed my arms. "This is psychotic."

Belmont's smile vanished, and his face bore a serious
glare. Had I said something to finally break his nerve? I
had said loads of disrespectful comments to him during
our last visit. His eyes darkened and his lips pulled back,
revealing his perfectly white false teeth.

"Now you listen, friend. You're here to feed, and I
will provide for you because I know of no other safe way
for you to do so. And since we can't have you running
wild and feeding at will, I'll continue to help. But since
you've joined me here in the room, there's no turning
back. You'll want to at first, but you'll need to control
your urge to run. Because the hunger will take over once
I've made the first stroke." Belmont reached beneath the
table and pulled out a black hacksaw.

It took several seconds to register his actions. I gaped in horror at the body and then at Belmont clutching the sharp tool. Before I could plead for him to stop, he dragged the blade across the man's skull, crudely opening the flesh just above the top of his head.

I stammered a few incoherent words and stumbled backward toward the door. I was too clumsy now. Ever since the incident, I almost always tripped on the slightest obstructions. My feet fumbled on the stone floor, and I toppled over in a heap beneath the gurney. Shielding my eyes, I covered my ears, trying to drown out the smooth sounds of a saw on bone.

Another stroke of saw blade cutting against wood, only it wasn't wood.

The tearing of flesh.

Thick bands of blood slowly dripped from the head.

A hollow, popping sound.

A moan. Someone had just moaned! I wouldn't have believed it, had I not heard it with my own ears.

I scampered backward, trying to flee the gruesome scene. Was the man still alive? Was Belmont murdering him right in front of me? My eyes darted up, and I saw the man's face, fearing I'd see his own eyes in pleading desperation. Instead, they were just the way I'd seen them before, closed behind dead eyelids. My eyes traveled higher to where Belmont's persistent sawing had opened a massive wound in the man's skull.

Another moan.

I wanted to throw up, but there was nothing inside of me to come out, nor did I think I could capably throw up out of my own disgust. Belmont must have been the one moaning. Not out of pain or sadness, but a moan of satisfaction.

I tried to turn for the door, but found the action too difficult.

Why did I want to stay?

Belmont finished working the blade and hovered over the incision, working his fingers beneath the skull. I caught sight of the brain, and my desire to leave whisked away once I caught a whiff of the most wonderful scent my nostrils had ever inhaled.

Brains.

More moaning erupted. And this time, it came from me.

# Chapter 9

When Belmont fed me the other night, I knew it was unlike any other meat I'd had in my life. The gelatinous texture, the stickiness, and the way it satisfied my hunger—nothing had ever made me feel that full, that complete. I should have known. I didn't want to believe it. But I had devoured the brains right out of a man's head, and I loved every bite. And now I prepared myself for another delicious meal.

The top of the man's head came off easier than I expected, and the brain nearly fell out. That was when I noticed the Y cut down the man's chest.

"*Most* bodies have been autopsied," Belmont started. "The pathologist removes all organs for examination and he or she weighs them. Once they're done, they put them in a neat little bag and place them back in the abdomen before they sew them up. Except for the brain. That goes back in the head." He pointed to the sutures around the top of the person's skull.

"Sick," I said. "Just sick."

Belmont broke the meat in half as if it were a loaf of

bread. I greedily sunk my teeth into it. Residual blood burst into my mouth like a ripe, plump tomato. I couldn't get enough. Bite after bite, I couldn't contain myself. Within a few minutes, it was gone, along with the high.

My chest heaved, and I realized I was out of breath from the frenzied eating. I sat on the floor, questioning what I'd just done, and stared at my hands.

They were still sticky.

"I know this was . . . a lot," Belmont said. "But you'll be expected to clean up next time. Watch carefully, and if you're up for it, you may help. Make no mistake, the cleanup is as important as the meal."

Belmont was a pro and went right to work clearing up the carnage. He produced a sponge and a bucket from beneath the washroom sink, filled it with soap and hot water, and then started in on the cleaning. I didn't want to watch, knowing what he was doing. What he was covering up. Last week, I was eating corn dogs and chicken fingers. My mom made spaghetti on Monday with garlic bread. Normal stuff. This wasn't normal. It was an abomination. I viciously wiped my hands against my jeans.

"Don't do that," Belmont grunted. He handed me a washrag, a bar of soap, and a bottle of antibacterial lotion. "Clean yourself up."

Belmont scrubbed the table beneath the man's head with the sponge and used a roll of paper towels to dry his handiwork.

"That's . . . a lot of blood." I gagged. "Seriously, why is there so much?"

"If you're going to vomit, please find a proper receptacle."

"Oh, puke is where you draw the line?" I asked. "Blood? Fine. Guts? No problem. Brains? Even better!"

"It's not the pathologist's job to drain them," Belmont sighed. "They leave that for the mortician during the embalming process."

"I see," I replied.

That man was just full of information he shouldn't have known.

After sloshing a mop across the floor for a few minutes beneath the gurney, he carried the bucket back to the washroom sink to empty the filthy water down the drain. Next, he covered the corpse with a white sheet and brought out an oscillating fan, directing its flow of air toward the wet floor. Then he opened a large garbage bag and dumped in the paper towels, the sponges, my bar of soap, and the washrags. He even removed the mop from off its handle and tossed that in as well.

Finally, after thoroughly inspecting what could only be labeled as a crime scene, Belmont washed his hands and arms up past his elbows in the sink with water so hot, steam billowed up from the faucet. Then he sprayed air freshener throughout the room until thick vapor filled the air. All so methodical, like a routine he had done countless times before. I shivered as I realized that he probably had.

He squatted beside me on the floor when he was finished. "Do you have a fireplace?" he asked.

"What?" My mind still felt clouded in a daze. His question had caught me off guard.

"A fireplace? At home?"

I shook my head at first and wiped my lips with the back of my hand. Belmont stared at me, waiting for my answer. "Yeah, we have a fireplace, I guess." I mean, we did, but who cared? Why was that important?

"You'll have to burn those now." He pointed to my blue jeans. "Once you've gone home and you're alone, burn your clothes. Everything."

"I barely know how to use it. And my parents will freak if they smell my clothes burning." My family hardly ever used it even in the winter. It was more of a decoration than anything else.

"You'll have to think of a good excuse. You don't have a choice, Calvin, not if you don't want to get caught. Your clothes will attract rats. Do you want rats infesting your bedroom?"

I made a pathetic whimper. "No." It was like this guy didn't think dumpsters were an option.

"Whenever you feed, you have to be thorough with your cleaning. Even though you cannot contract diseases, it doesn't mean no one else will. Our food can be deadly for others. Blood . . . brains . . ."

"All right! I got it!" I snapped.

"We have to be careful. Our kind isn't accepted into any circles of society. We must leave no trace. No evidence."

I looked at Belmont more closely now. His features seemed even more obvious than before. His face had been tailored in a way to conceal his true identity. Fake teeth, fake hair, contact lenses, and makeup. How long had he lived this way of life?

"Our kind?" I asked, swallowing. "There are more of us? More . . . zombies?" No point in skirting the issue anymore. I just chowed down on the memories of some dead guy, and instead of repulsion, my stomach felt an amazing sense of satisfaction. I, Calvin Simmons, was a zombie. The sooner I accepted that truth, the sooner I'd be able to discover a way to cure it.

Belmont stood, stretching. His body had withstood time and decomposition. Even from up close, despite knowing what I did about his true self, he looked normal.

From a distance, I could see no signs of anything out of the ordinary. I stared down at my own hands.

Gray.

My skin had turned gray, and not a subtle discoloration either. Standing alone in a hallway, maybe I could've passed as a regular, albeit sickly, kid. Standing next to any one of my classmates at Werner High, the difference would be obvious. The skin beneath my fingernails had become a shade of deep blue, almost purple. This had to be fixed. I needed to know what Belmont knew and how to adapt. Otherwise, people were bound to discover the monster I had become.

"There are more of us," Belmont said, answering my question. "I don't know how many, but there are others." He noticed a smudge of brain residue on the edge of the gurney. Without hesitation, he covered the distance to the washroom sink and returned with a paper towel and a spray bottle of disinfectant.

"Where are they?" I asked, staring down at my rotting hands as Belmont attacked the spot with the cleanser. "Why haven't I seen them before—you know, like on the news?" This type of stuff was what people went nuts over. Seriously, a race of undead corpses. We flocked to theaters to watch them. You would think if there were others surviving in the world, someone in the media would've eventually learned of their existence.

"Most of the ones that are left are exactly like you and me. They have learned to adapt. To fit in and go unnoticed. Many years ago, that wasn't the case. It was harder." Belmont helped me to my feet. "We can't stay here much longer."

"How did they get like this? Does this happen all the time?" I turned away from the white mass of the dead man beneath the sheet, no longer wishing to think about him.

Belmont smiled faintly. "No, you're the first I've known of in quite some time."

"And it was because of that stone in the mausoleum?"

Belmont nodded.

"Well, is there a way to use that stone to turn me . . . turn us back?" I asked, desperate. Now that I felt full, I couldn't bear thinking of feasting on another man's brain. I knew, however, that once the hunger returned, that would be a different story.

Belmont frowned. "The zombie effects are irreversible."

Just like that, he had squashed any inkling of hope. Snuffed it right out like a withering candle wick. For now, I would accept this. I was too full to argue. Maybe Belmont understood how to live, and maybe he had exhausted all his resources in search of a cure, but nothing was absolute. Science had proven that time and time again. There would be a way to fix me, and I was determined to find it.

Belmont gave one last perusal around the gurney to ensure we had covered our tracks. "Time to go."

"What'll happen to him?" I pointed at the dead man.

"The son—who works at the morgue—he'll be by soon to take him back there. The bodies can only be taken and returned in a short window before someone from a funeral home comes for transport."

"And no one notices? Not even the funeral director?"

"If they did, this little arrangement wouldn't work." Belmont paused, and I assumed he sensed I wasn't satisfied. "The mortician won't notice, no. I cut in the same spot the coroner did. I'm very careful."

"And he doesn't care about what you did?"

"Who? Him?" Confused, Belmont nodded toward the body.

"No," I spat. "Your creepy pal from the morgue. While you go about eating people's brains? He doesn't care that you did this?" How could anyone turn a blind eye to that?

"We did this, Calvin, *we* did this," Belmont corrected. "And no, Samuel doesn't care, because he's unaware of what happens here after he leaves." He clicked off the flashlight and hid it in one of the cupboards along the wall.

"How can he not know? What if he called the police? How would he explain what goes on here? That you're selling the brains on the black market?"

"For science." Belmont opened the door leading to the alley and exited.

That didn't make any sense. I nearly tripped over Belmont as he bent down to return the key to its home beneath the muddy boot.

"I told him my profession is in the field of neurobiology." Belmont's voice sounded much lower than when he stood inside the safety of the building. "I'm a brain scientist, but unfortunately, I've been out of work as of late. Since I want to stay fresh in my field as I pursue other career options, I've explained to him my need of materials. Brains aren't something I can just pick up at the local thrift store. I tell Samuel that I use them for scientific research. He doesn't question it, partly because I pay him an exorbitant amount of money to keep his mouth shut and to not ask questions, but also because why would he ever think anyone in their right mind would do such atrocious things to a human brain?"

"It's because we're not in our right minds, are we?" I asked.

"No, we are not," Belmont admitted with a shrug. "Of course, it's illegal to steal property from the dead's relatives, thus the reasoning behind our little cloak-and-dagger operation. Samuel makes the delivery whenever business presents itself to the mortuary."

"You mean whenever someone dies?"

Belmont seemed to be growing annoyed with my constant badgering. "Look, I understand your concern. This is all new and exciting to you . . ."

"Exciting?" I interjected.

He held up a hand, trying to calm me. "Not the best choice of words, but you know what I mean. No matter how alarming or frightening this may be, this practice is a much better solution to our predicament than eating the brains of the living. I trust you can agree with me on that."

We walked away from the direction of the Cobalt, out the side I left a few nights before, and headed toward the sleeping industrial zone.

All of it was bizarre. Probably not the best word for it, but it would do for now.

Bizarre.

I wondered what kind of guy Samuel was. A vision of a thirty-something-year-old man flooded into my mind, probably single and odd-looking, driving a long station wagon around town with dead bodies covered in sheets in the trunk. I guess living as a zombie didn't give too many options of how to find food. The situation probably forced Belmont to associate with some interesting individuals.

"Okay," I blurted out after we had walked for over ten minutes in silence. I sped up my pace to join Belmont at his side. "What do you do if someone doesn't die for a while? I mean, this is Jewkes—people just don't die all the time here. It can be weeks or longer."

"Jefferson isn't far and has a population of almost two hundred thousand. Plenty of people die on a regular basis. But it's true, there have been times when the deceased don't come so readily." Belmont slowed and faced me. "We have three days to find food. That's the amount of time it takes before the hunger truly kicks in between feedings now that you've completely turned. After a week, we've hit a dangerous position. You cannot push your limits. If you've not eaten before a week, you're in grave danger. At that point, I have a few plan Bs."

Did I really want to know what they were? I asked anyway. "Like what?"

"I've made many trips over the years to the university in the neighboring town of Chidester to visit the anatomy labs where they store the cadavers."

"You've got to be kidding me."

Belmont bared his teeth, raising his eyebrows in what might have been embarrassment.

"Yuck!" Yeah, I just said yuck, which didn't make a whole heap of sense seeing as how I had just dined on brain, but for some reason, munching on a cadaver . . . it just didn't sit well with me.

"It's not the best meal," he said with regret. "Think of your worst cafeteria experience, douse it with a bunch of chemicals, and multiply that by ten, then you may have an idea. But those brains will satisfy your hunger, and that is all that matters. You cannot allow yourself to lose control. Terrible, terrible things happen if you do."

"You keep saying that. I get it. I must eat. Everyone does, but what terrible things will happen if I don't? Will I die like any normal human being?" Dying wasn't the end of the world if I really looked at the alternative. Living for brains.

"No, you will not die, but you will eat," Belmont replied gravely. "And you will find food in whatever way you can."

"From a cow or a horse or something like that? Will I eat dog brains?" I still couldn't believe I was having this conversation.

"What happens now when you eat food? Regular food?" Belmont asked.

"I throw it up. All of it."

Belmont looked upon me as though preparing me for some terrible news. "Brains are the only substance that will satisfy your hunger. Nothing else will. And they can't come from any other living creature. They have to be raw, preferably not overly rotten, and they have to come from a human."

He seemed to always prolong the explanation, as though he'd rather I figured it out for myself. Annoying, but it worked. I finally got it. If I didn't find a dead body to eat before a week passed, I would end up killing somebody for their brain. I could never let that happen.

Belmont and I looked at each other for a moment, and I sensed he understood I had grasped it.

"Is it like it is in the movies?" I asked. "Will I chase people down and attack them?"

"Let's not talk about this."

"No, I want to talk about it."

"Once you've reached the point of no return, a change will come over your entire body. We call it the rage, and there's nothing you can do to stop it. You'll lose all sense of who you really are and will attack anyone that crosses your path to appease that hunger." Belmont paused, studying my eyes. "You mustn't let yourself go that long."

More questions swarmed my mind. "If I kill somebody and eat their brain, will they come back as a zombie as well?"

Although I couldn't see his face, I sensed his frowning. "You have to be careful now. Any significant contact you have with another individual's blood will spread the infection."

"Be a gem and define significant contact," I said.

"You are a carrier of a disease. If that disease enters the bloodstream of another person, they can and most likely will contract the condition."

"So, no biting," I said. "Hey, what about making out?" That was an important query.

"This is not a joking matter. There's no going back from this. Don't take it lightly."

"Oh, I won't," I insisted. "But what about kissing?" I needed an answer. I might not want to go on living, period, if I couldn't kiss.

Belmont rubbed his eyes with his fingers. "Why do you want to know?"

"Because I want to kiss a girl, and if you keep saying I can live a normal life, but I can't hook up with anybody, then I think you're full of it!"

Belmont considered this. "I suppose kissing would not spread the disease. That is unless the person you're kissing has an open wound in their mouth."

I considered this for a moment. *Jaylen!* I hadn't bitten him, or bled on him, so he was probably fine. I thought about mentioning this to Belmont but . . . he seemed paranoid. I made a mental note to check on Jaylen the next time I saw him, before I involved Belmont.

"What about that dude back there on the slab?" My

voice rose with excitement. "There was direct bloodstream contact! He's not going to jump up and start hanging out with us too, is he?"

Belmont shook his head. "Just like a normal human, the zombie's brain is its link to life. Without that organ, all creatures cease to exist. We've destroyed the man's brain, so he won't be coming back."

I felt slightly relieved. Only slightly.

"I've heard, or at least seen in the movies, that zombies are dumb and they keep going after people and don't stop no matter what. We're not like that at all, right?"

Belmont began walking again, and this time I kept up with his stride. "We're not like that now, because we're in control of our faculties. When a zombie is no longer in control, they'll act differently, but maybe not like in the movies. Of course, if someone blows off your kneecap with a shotgun or rearranges your head with a sledgehammer, it might slow you down a bit. But it won't stop you."

"Basically, don't go hungry for a week and that won't happen, right?" I asked.

Belmont appeared to consider telling me something more, but then thought better of it. I could see it in his mannerisms. Something he wanted to explain to me, but probably didn't feel I could handle. My thoughts didn't dwell longer on his elusiveness. Instead, I thought about the brains again.

"Brains are my only meal option?" I so wanted this to be Belmont's stab at humor, but he didn't cave. "Can we cook them? Mix them up in a casserole or grill them?"

"That won't work."

"Can I put them between a bun with some mustard just so it looks normal?" I was clinging to the ledge with this argument. Searching for any scrap of hope.

"I suppose if you wanted, you could. But the bread won't remain in your digestive track. Besides, when we eat, the carnal nature of our condition takes over. A feeding zombie has no desire for anything but to satisfy his hunger for brains. Which means you won't be looking for any other ingredients whenever you eat."

Belmont halted in front of an old, rundown meat-processing factory. The faded gray moniker above the delivery bay doors read "Herman Cuts." The windows had been boarded up, with huge chains draped across the entry doors. "This is where I live," he said.

"You live here? In there?" I asked, not even attempting to mask my astonishment.

Belmont walked toward the building to where one of the window boards had been loosened and the rusty, bent nails littered the ground beneath.

"Why would you live here? I thought you said we needed to fit in."

"And *you* will. With some adjustments and practice, I can help you live a somewhat normal life." After he peeled back the board, I peered in through the window. Below in the room, I spotted a mattress lying on the stone floor with a few blankets, a sleeping bag, and several pillows. A mirror hung on the wall over a small stand cluttered with various jars of makeup and cosmetics. Stacks of newspapers and what looked like schoolbooks rested on the floor beside the mattress, with one of the books opened facedown on the bed pillow.

"You sleep in there every night?" Sorry, but his place was a dump! If that was living a normal life, I'd gladly pass.

"I don't sleep, and neither do you. We don't need it anymore. But it is better to lie down every night and be still. Moving around is dangerous for us, particularly in the dark. Our bodies don't heal in a normal fashion. Your arm is an example of that. I can fix the bone so that it doesn't reappear above the skin, but the bone itself will never fuse back together."

"You mean this thing is broken forever?" I gaped down at my arm, unsure of what to think. It would never be whole again.

"I'm sorry, but now imagine if it were your leg or your neck. Can you see why it's important to take care of yourself? A broken bone in those regions of your body will make it more than just a little awkward to move around, don't you think? You'll need to come up with a way to avoid any follow-up appointments with your doctor, or they'll be very suspicious." Sticking his feet through the window, he shimmied down to a ladder below. "Meet me here tomorrow night around eleven. Can you do that?"

"I think so."

"Good." He nodded. "We'll get started on your improvements."

"You mean like a wig and false teeth and stuff like that, huh?" I ducked down as the headlights of an approaching car cut through the darkness and sped past the factory.

Belmont lowered his body all the way through the window and disappeared for a moment. When he returned, he handed me up an aerosol can.

I held it so that I could make out the name of the can from the glare of the streetlights.

"Abram's Industrial Strength Deodorizer. What am I going to use this for?"

"It's one of the most powerful cleansers on the market. The sanitation department uses it to shield the smell of construction outhouses during relocation. I've discovered it to be quite useful in fooling even the most ultrasensitive olfactory organs around." He offered me a pleasant smile.

"You just made absolutely no sense whatsoever." I scratched my head and turned the aerosol can over to try and read the back.

Belmont chuckled. "I think you can discover a few ways to use that on your own."

"One more question," I said.

Belmont paused from going back into the factory. "Yes."

I smiled. "Are we the running type of zombies or the walking type of zombies?"

"Whatever you want," Belmont answered. "To answer your question . . . I guess both."

"So sophisticated-type zombies."

# Chapter 10

First order of business, check on Jaylen. I had decided to confront him in homeroom without revealing my current status—since he didn't believe it anyway. "So you're saying I'm less stinky?" I asked.

"I can't smell you from here, so it's an improvement," Jaylen said.

"Smell me." I lifted my armpit in his direction.

"Sick!" He crossed his fingers in front of him like a rosary. "Guys don't sniff guys."

I thought back to my conversation with Belmont. Jaylen seemed normal enough, though I couldn't tell if he smelled or not.

"Has anyone mentioned you stink?" I stuffed my hands in my pockets.

"What? Naw, man. I'm always fresh." He smiled. "Stop being weird."

"How have you been feeling? Any vomiting fits?"

He crossed his arms and didn't answer.

"I'll take that as a no."

"What's with you? Is this another joke, like the

night we played video games?" Jaylen stayed seated but splayed out his legs and arms, pretending to walk in place. "No . . ." He lowered his voice and drew out his words. "I don't have a sleepwalking disease."

"Very funny." I tried to laugh it off. "How's the scratch?"

"Oh this?" Jaylen rolled up his shorts and removed a large white gauze. "Definitely going to leave a scar. Official story is I fought off a wolverine."

Blood still oozed from it. Good! That was a good sign. I didn't bleed, not that I'd seen. Jaylen was fine. I hadn't turned him.

"Did I hear you talking about Calvin reeking?" Shelby walked by. "Thanks for finally showering. You were stinking up the whole class."

"Sorry about that." I waved her off. "Hey, wait a minute, how does Jaylen smell?"

Jaylen shot me an angry glance. Shelby leaned down, just inches from his neck. He shivered. I knew he liked her. He should be thanking me!

"He smells nice, like the ocean." She stood, then looked at me. "Seriously, you were gross. Can you try not to assault my nose ever again?"

I nodded, hoping she'd go away.

Abram's Industrial Strength Deodorizer.

What a wonderful creation. I started spraying the stuff all over me on the walk back home, and man was it the ticket. My parents backed off with their complaints, and I was able to go back to school.

I even had a few girls flirt with me. Or let me flirt with them. True, I had turned into an undead zombie that feasted upon dead people's brains, but this was high school, man. Tons of kids my age who hung out in the hallways looked worse than death and involved themselves in far more deviant extracurricular activities. Things were definitely looking up. Of course, Belmont explained the spray would only work in the early stages of decomposition, which was what my body was doing. It could make a wicked Halloween costume.

I'd spent a little time each day trying out different foods, but nothing stayed down. It didn't matter if it was highly processed or as simple as a sack of lettuce—it all came up. There had to be *something* I could eat besides brains. I was confident I'd find a way to eat again. I'd just need time. Lucky for me, I had all the time in the world.

I kept my appointment with Belmont the following night.

Laid out on a table were all sorts of goodies. A wig that was pretty dang close to my hair brought me the most relief.

"Dang, where'd you get all this stuff? Dentures?" I picked up the gleaming white set of teeth. "My teeth are fine."

"For now," Belmont said. "At some point, they're going to start falling out. Once that commences, we'll need to remove them all at once and replace. It's better to have these things on hand then scramble to get them last minute."

"My parents spent all that money on braces for noth-ing." I tapped on a metal plate. "And this?"

"Titanium, for your arm. That's the priority. Then, we'll shave your head and suture the wig onto it. As I said, the dentures can wait. But"—he held my chin and stared into my eyes—"the contacts cannot. Your eyes are looking extremely gray and faded."

I couldn't stand to watch him fish around in the hole in my arm, or when he filleted it open and screwed the metal plate to my bone. Even for me, in my state, it seemed too gruesome. Though I didn't bleed, so that was a plus.

"Whoa, what did you put over my skin to make it look so smooth?" I stared at my perfectly normal-looking arm. "Is this some sort of magic?"

"If you had been paying attention, you would have learned how to repair injuries. And trust me, you're going to need to learn."

"Okay, what's next?" I asked.

Belmont held a pair of clippers. "Since it won't grow back, there's no need to pull it from the root. Eventually the tiny follicles still left will simply fall out."

I stared in the mirror as Belmont glided the clippers over my skull. I expected it to tickle but the sensation never came. My bald head was paler than I ever imagined. Either from lack of sun, or the whole being dead thing, I didn't care. It needed to be covered up immediately.

"Here." Belmont handed me the wig. "It's easier to start with your head down. Place the top of it flush with your forehead and swing your head back. Then bring the open ends together in the back."

I did as he instructed. This was all so weird—wigs, contacts, surgery in a basement.

"Okay, looks pretty good." I looked at my gray reflection in the mirror as Belmont fixed the back. "You'll show me how to do that, right?"

"Yes." Belmont sighed. "You have a lot of things to learn today. This can wait a few days. It'll stay on and tight for at least a week. Can you put in contacts?"

"Probably, I've seen it done before."

The flimsy contact lens easily stuck to my eyeball. I was thankful I couldn't feel because that sucker would have irritated the crap out of me premortem.

Belmont handed me a spongy triangle and a bottle of liquid foundation.

"Squirt a few pumps onto the top of your hand and dip the sponge into it." Belmont did the same on his hand. "Don't drag it across your face. Use more of a tapping motion."

His gray pallor disappeared behind the makeup. I did the same and watched my complexion improve vastly. I moved to the other exposed skin on my neck and hands. Then I finished it with some sort of setting powder and just a touch of blush.

"Never thought I'd be wearing makeup." I laughed.

"Many men wear makeup these days, it's very progressive," Belmont said. "Final item on the agenda today is embalming."

"Embalming?" I asked. "No one's going to pump liquid Drano into my veins."

"Well, if you don't want your skin to fall off, then you're going to need it done monthly."

A monthly embalming wasn't the recreational activity I had hoped to have for the rest of my life.

"How long does it take? This embalming?"

"About an hour or two, depending how much clotting has gone on in your body," Belmont explained. "A normal human body decomposes pretty rapidly, but for us, it's much different. Slower and more drawn out. It's because only parts of your body are decomposing. A zombie still needs most of its organs to survive. The process is more of a transformation than a rotting, so to speak. Your hair and teeth have only loosened in their roots, and other than some of your unnecessary inner organs dying off, like your appendix and gallbladder, you just have a bit of an unnatural smell."

"Yeah, but thanks to my Abram's deodorant, I've got

that under wraps." I sniffed my armpit for good measure. Couldn't smell anything, but I thought the gesture appropriate.

"For now," Belmont agreed. "But the smell will become more repulsive over the next week, and even the spray won't cover it. You'll start to attract flies and other insects. They'll cling to you like a piece of rotted fruit. Your skin is not a necessary organ for sustainment in a zombie, and most of it will start to rot. You'll lose parts of your eyes and gums, not to mention the pus that will replace your blood . . ."

"All right, all right, I get it! Enough with the pus!" I gagged. "How do you do this, and what does it involve?"

"I've performed it on myself for many years intravenously. The typical chemicals used in embalming a body for burial are not enough. We need a higher concentration. This will involve a stronger mixture of formaldehyde and other chemicals generally used to preserve cadavers. The universities use it quite frequently. Trust me, it won't hurt, and you'll be grateful you did it."

First thing he did was stick the fattest needle I've ever seen into an artery above my right collarbone and another tube into my jugular vein. I used to have this thing where I nearly passed out whenever I saw a needle about to stick into my skin. A kind of sissy trait that didn't win me any macho points, but I got it from my mom. Despite my condition, I watched the whole embalming process and found it fascinating.

"Dang, that stuff looks thick." A machine pumped amber-colored liquid into me.

"I'm not going to drain your blood. It's unnecessary."

"Why?"

"Is everything a quiz with you?" Belmont rubbed his forehead. "You don't have much left. Remember how you didn't bleed during the repair of your arm? And what little blood is left, we need for your organs."

"Oh, right." I touched the thick tubing delivering the chemicals to my veins. "That whole thing."

I was only momentarily distracted when he opened a drawer and I saw a glimpse of an old-timey photo. Like the ones you saw in tourist traps. The family was wearing historical clothes, and the whole thing was sepia toned. I wanted to ask about it, but Belmont was laser focused.

We needed my muscles and tendons to absorb the embalming fluid in order to slow the rotting process. Apparently, I had quite a bit of clotting, because my embalming took close to four hours. But when we finished, I was a brand-new man. My skin felt full and healthy, and my eyes didn't seem as gaunt and sunken.

*Yep, folks, embalming. I highly recommend it, but only if you're a zombie.*

***

On Saturday evening, my dad's work gave him a rare night off, so he opted to take my mom out for Chinese food. Since I had nothing else to do, with all my homework caught up and nothing worth watching on the television, I grabbed my bike and rode the seven miles into town to meet Belmont.

I found him propped up against several pillows on his bed, reading a thick textbook. When I rapped on his window with my knuckles, he nearly fell off the bed.

"You shouldn't startle me like that," he said, annoyed. "And what are you doing here so early? It's not wise for us to meet during the day when people could see." He held the ladder while I climbed down.

"Relax. I was home all by myself and thought an

early dinner would be sweet. And there's a movie on at midnight that I want to watch." I noticed a shiny spot of liquid bandage on Belmont's shoulder, and then looked past him into the next room, where the embalming equipment appeared recently used.

"That's fine, I suppose, but going forward, we stick to schedule. No surprises." Belmont seemed uneasy. Irritated.

"What were you reading?" I glanced at the overturned textbook.

"No need for you to know," he responded.

Since I didn't really care, I didn't press the issue. Belmont took the next fifteen minutes to ready himself to go out. After he applied his makeup and checked the part in his sutured hair, we climbed the ladder and headed out for the alley.

"Hey, what was that picture in your desk?"

"Excuse me?" Belmont raised an eyebrow in my direction. "It's rude to look in other people's drawers. If it's not on display, there's a reason."

"I was just asking because I was wondering if it was your family." I cringed, realizing my misstep. I tried to recover the best I could. "I mean, we have pics like that too. My parents took us on a lame vacation to South Dakota and ended up in Wall Drug—you know what I'm talking about. There are billboards for it everywhere. Anyway, I was thinking maybe you'd been there too and gotten your dumb pics like we did."

"No." Belmont's entire mood had shifted from mad to sad, then back to mad. "It's been a good deal since I've seen my family."

It hit me how lonely Belmont must be. He had distanced himself from family, that was obvious. Or maybe he outlived them? He only looked to be in his forties, but then again . . . best to drop it or I might not eat tonight.

Our dinner that night tasted far better than my first two meals. A twenty-four-year-old female from Hyde Park who died from a drug overdose. Her neighbors found her sprawled across her overturned television set nearly two days after.

"Are you sure this is safe?" I poked at the gray matter. "Like, I won't overdose, will I?"

"No." Belmont attempted to roll his eyes.

"Will it show up in a drug test? My dad is *always* convinced I'm on drugs."

"I'm happy to eat without you." Belmont bit into his half of the small brain.

I hesitated, but couldn't resist. But I did wait a second to make sure Belmont didn't keel over.

"Here goes nothing." I sunk my teeth into the brain.

Her brain, though small and slightly chewy, tasted like top sirloin and mashed potatoes. At least, those were the closest flavors I could imagine. I closed my eyes and savored the moment. The dirty, bloody, sticky moment.

Belmont seemed distant, annoyed still by my sudden appearance. Perhaps he wasn't used to someone else breaking up his routine. Sorry, but who died and made him head zombie? Or maybe it was a combination of that and me peppering him with questions about his family. I suppose I'd be salty if I left my family . . . or rather *when*.

We began the cleanup, with him only speaking to bark out simple instructions. Where to find replacement mop heads, which sanitizer spray to use on the gurney, and how long to hold the sponges under the scalding hot water before sloshing them across the floor. I didn't object as long as I didn't have to handle the cleaning around the body. My stomach felt full and satisfied, and I would be home with plenty of time to watch my movie.

While fitting the sheet back over the girl, I heard something make a sound in the mudroom.

"What was that?" I whispered.

"Did you lock the door?" Belmont asked, his eyes wide and panicked.

"Why was I supposed to lock the door? This is only my second time here!" I didn't know Belmont had given me the assignment of door security, but I wished I had at least thought to lock it.

Belmont held a finger to his lips.

Images of police officers called to check out strange behavior entered my mind. They would find us with bits of brain dribbling from our chins and a hollow-headed corpse. *Dateline*, get ready. We were going to be the stars of some awful program.

"Could it be the owners?" I tried to keep my voice low, but the anxiety was killing me . . . and I was already dead. Belmont swatted a hand at me to silence my questions, and I clamped my own hand over my mouth. Slowly and ever so quietly, the two of us opened the door wide enough to see into the next room.

Someone in a gray hooded sweatshirt leapt over an overturned box of pamphlets, bounding for the exit. At first, I just figured it to be Belmont's delivery guy, Samuel, who still would have presented a problem to us in explaining what we were doing, but at least he knew there would be someone here operating on a body. But then I recognized the Werner High logo on the intruder's back, and his all-too-familiar black, bald head poking out from under the hood.

"Jaylen! Stop!" I shouted. But Jaylen wanted no part of it.

Climbing the stairs in a fury, he grappled with the doorknob of the exit before violently wrenching it open. I stood frozen in place, unsure of how to proceed. Should I chase after him? Belmont didn't have any trouble moving, and before I could react, he had crossed the length of floor between the room and exit, swinging the mop like a dangerous weapon.

Though athletic and one of the fastest base runners in the county, Jaylen must have been running in a state of alarm and not thinking clearly. When he saw Belmont on his tail, he stumbled and only made it halfway out of the building before Belmont fell on him. Jaylen had youth and strength, but Belmont possessed a frightening determination. Within moments, Jaylen was pinned to the ground, his chest beneath Belmont's knees. Belmont had the end of the mop handle raised above his head, prepared to drive it through Jaylen's skull. I came to my senses.

"Belmont, no!" I screamed, running over to intercept. I grabbed hold of the mop and felt his strength bearing down on my best friend. Had I not reacted when I did, he would've killed Jaylen.

"Don't hurt me, please! I won't tell anybody, I swear!" he begged.

"What are you doing here?" I asked.

Jaylen gasped for air as Belmont's knees weighed down heavily on his chest. "Ah, man, I just . . . I followed you! I was riding with my sister when I saw you and that guy walking. So I thought I'd see what you were up to."

"Big mistake!" Belmont snapped.

"No kidding," Jaylen said. "Look, I didn't mean to sneak up on you guys. Just let me go and . . . and . . . I'll just pretend . . ."

"Where's Heather?" I looked to the door, expecting

to see Jaylen's sister peering through the opening. Belmont pointed to the door, and I raced over to slam it shut.

"Buying some junk," Jaylen said. "At some . . . uh . . . cosmetics store a couple blocks over, but she's going to pick me up . . . soon. The store has probably already closed for the night."

I could see the desperation in his eyes as he searched for a way out of this. We didn't have much time to squash this problem. More people would be entering the scene, and if Jaylen could raise the alarm, Heather was ten times worse.

"What did you see?" Belmont demanded. He still had the mop primed and ready to puncture Jaylen, but I closed my fingers around the handle and managed to pry it from his hand.

"Nothing!" Jaylen repeated. He started to chuckle, trying to play it off. "I just barely walked in. Like two minutes ago. I didn't see anything . . . I swear."

"Don't lie to me," Belmont hissed.

"Let him up," I said, pulling on Belmont's shoulders.

"Not until he tells me the truth. Do you hear that? You lie to me, I kill you. And then I'll go to the cosmetics store and kill your sister, Heather, too."

"Geez, man!" I said, unable to believe what I was hearing. Belmont had never shown me this sort of aggression. Where was it coming from? Would he really kill Jaylen? The image of him poised to strike with the mop handle flashed into my head and I knew he would.

The smile erased from Jaylen's face, and he continued to breathe in quick bursts. "Okay, I saw things. I thought maybe it was a mannequin or something. But then I saw . . . whatever. But what you two do is your business. I don't need to know."

"What sort of things did you see?" Belmont pressed.

I felt an anvil crushing against my chest. Jaylen had seen me scooping up dinner from that girl. My high school life had ended.

Jaylen blinked. He stared at Belmont and then at me, his eyes wild and terrified. "I saw what you did . . . in there." He pointed back to the room where the body of the overdosed woman lay slightly covered by a sheet. "I saw . . ." He started laughing, but it seemed uncontrolled. If he didn't get a handle on himself, Jaylen would break into a fit of hysterics.

"Relax," I coaxed. "Take a breath."

Jaylen's eyes snapped toward mine and his laughter stopped. "Take a breath? Is that what I'm supposed to do? Calvin, you and your new buddy here just ate a woman! Why did you do that?" he shouted. "How? How could you?"

My chest heaved. I passed my fingers through my newly sutured hair, trying to think of a good explanation, but could only draw blanks.

"It's not what you think, Jaylen. Let him up." I pulled once again on Belmont's shoulder, and this time he obeyed. He slowly released his hold and stood up. Jaylen just lay there, unsure of his next move.

"I tried to tell you a couple of days ago, but you thought I was kidding. Now do you believe me?" I asked.

Jaylen gave a few sideways glances toward the door, but remained on the floor. "Yeah, I guess, but you never said you were eating dead bodies!"

"I have no choice. And we're not eating the bodies. Just . . ." Really? Was I really going to share this tidbit? "Just the brains." I guess I was.

Jaylen groaned and covered his eyes with the backs of his hands. "Brains? No, no, no, no. No!" He dug his fingers below his eyelids, threatening to pluck them out. "You don't do that. You really shouldn't. You . . . you . . ."

He was losing it. I could see where this was headed. Jaylen needed an intervention, and by the looks of Belmont, he would be no help.

"I've changed," I said, my voice shaking but somewhat in control. "I'm still the same Calvin, but I have a new diet."

Belmont smirked. "Clever."

I nudged him out of the way, hoping the removal of his daunting presence would ease Jaylen's tension.

"You kill people now?" Jaylen whispered.

"No!" I answered, shaking my head. "It's not like that. They're already dead when they're delivered. And their families never know what happened. We just have to eat, and this is the only way we can."

Jaylen slowly sat up and looked awkwardly at Belmont, who didn't look ready to chum it up. His eyes bore seriousness, a mixture of anger and concern.

"What's your next move? Jaylen, is it?" Belmont asked, reaching over and offering a hand. Jaylen didn't take it.

"Next move?" he asked. "What do you mean?"

Belmont retracted his hand and folded his arms at his chest. He glanced at me, as if calculating something in his mind. I had no idea what to do, or what I should say. He took a deep breath and slowly released it through his nostrils. Then he turned to me and shook his head morosely. "Calvin, we can't let him go."

I heard him, but the words took a little longer to register. My mind kept replaying the moment when we entered the mudroom an hour earlier, but instead, I inserted a memory of me locking the deadbolt on the door. Why didn't I think to do that? This was my fault. I could've prevented all of this.

"Can't let him go?" I asked, finally grasping it.

"He's seen way too much. He'll talk."

"No, I won't!" Jaylen chimed in. "I'm not a snitch! I won't tell anybody!"

Belmont ignored his ramblings. "When that happens, even as ridiculous as it will sound coming from him, someone will believe it. The rumor will spread, and we won't be safe. Things like this have happened to me before."

"What did you do then?" I asked, kneeling next to Jaylen. "Did you kill them?"

Belmont stared at me, unblinking. "Survival is key."

"I swear on my life and my family's life and my dog's life and my girlfriend's life . . ."

"Your girlfriend's life?" I suppressed a laugh.

"Oh, heck yeah! Moira? I'd swear on her in a heartbeat! Anything you want. I don't want any trouble. I'll keep my mouth shut."

I helped Jaylen to his feet, and the two of us stood next to each other. Things had changed a lot in the past week, and I doubted we'd ever be the same again.

"You're just saying these things to save your neck. Everyone does. It's a natural reaction to these circumstances." Belmont picked up the mop stick but didn't hold it threateningly. Instead, he walked back into the room. Jaylen and I stood there silently. He wouldn't look at me, but I didn't think I could look at him either. When Belmont returned, Jaylen brought his hands up, clenched in fists, ready for the worst.

"You'll talk, but maybe no one will believe you," Belmont said.

"Maybe he should talk," I said, my voice cracking at first.

Jaylen nodded. "Yeah, right—what?" he asked turning to look at me.

Belmont mimicked his action. "You think he should talk?"

It didn't sound so smart coming out of my mouth, but I had an idea. "Yes. Like you said, who's going to believe him? And if we make him promise not to, he will." Jaylen looked ready to protest, but I cut him off. "You will, man. You've got a big mouth, and you gossip more than an old lady."

Jaylen flinched, but then grinned. "At least I don't eat brains."

We laughed, but I still knew it wouldn't last. I needed to explain everything to Jaylen. I needed him to support me at least for a little while. Belmont agreed, and I took the next fifteen minutes to fill Jaylen in on everything that had happened—from the man who attacked me in the mausoleum, to my first brain-meal encounter, to the process of embalming and the Abrams Industrial Strength Deodorizer. With Belmont providing backup to all my information, Jaylen caught on to the situation a lot quicker than I could've hoped. Though I was pretty sure Belmont had done an excellent job of scaring him to death.

"You're a zombie?" Jaylen asked after I was done explaining.

"Yes," I answered.

"Like in the movies?"

"Not exactly."

Belmont went to the door to look out for Jaylen's sister while I showed him the woman on the gurney.

"See?"

"Is this real?" Jaylen gagged. "How can you stand the smell!"

"I can't smell."

"Oh." Jaylen shrugged, his eyes fixated on the body.

"It's not like we killed her. She was already dead. It's like, the ultimate form of recycling."

"Whoa." Jaylen circled the body. "This is wild. But she's so young, how'd she . . ."

"OD'd."

"This is wild."

"I'm not evil or anything like that," I said. "Belmont has shown me how to adjust. To live a somewhat normal life. But I have to eat like this."

Jaylen's face strained in a half-smile. "No more pizza, or chips?" I shook my head. "What about the other night when we ate those nachos?"

"Gone. All of it. I threw it all up in the bathroom throughout the night, just like I told you."

Jaylen laughed.

"Your sister is here, parked at the end of the alley," Belmont announced, moving away from the window. "You'd better go before she grows suspicious."

Jaylen nodded. "So how's this going to work?"

I shrugged. "You go home, and then maybe you can come over tomorrow to my place and we can talk about it more if you want."

"Yeah, cool. I won't tell anybody." He looked at Belmont. "I promise, dude."

Jaylen left. Heather's car pulled away from the curb, and Belmont and I exited the building. I still could feel the anxiety gnawing on my insides, but I felt good about Jaylen.

"You see? It'll be all right," I said as Belmont and I began our walk back to his place. "Jaylen gets it now. He'll keep quiet. You'll see."

Back at Belmont's, I grabbed my bike and straddled the seat. He still hadn't spoken since we left the alley.

"Is everything going to be okay?" I asked.

Belmont looked at me and stroked his chin. "I don't know, Calvin."

"You were there. You heard him. He seemed legit. Don't you think?"

Belmont gave a half shrug with his shoulders. "Perhaps. And if he doesn't keep quiet, be prepared to say goodbye to everyone for good. We'll need to relocate. And finding another person like Samuel is nearly impossible. To be honest, I think your friend Jaylen will end up changing everything for the worst."

# Chapter 11

Jaylen kept his word. If anything, our friendship, which had been pretty good before, grew stronger. Now we had something else to talk about other than baseball, video games, and girls. My condition fascinated Jaylen, and we spent many afternoons reviewing tape. Meaning, we watched every zombie flick we could get our hands on. From *Night of the Living Dead* and all the sequels to *Thriller* and newer material.

I couldn't stand the ones with the dumb zombies, dragging their feet in the road behind them. Belmont and I proved that to be bunk. The movies with zombies able to charge and leap and use logic to solve problems turned out to be the scariest movies for me. As I watched those, I couldn't help but think about what would happen if I missed a meal for too long.

Along with Jaylen's fascination about my "zombie-ness"—his word, not mine—he continually asked questions about Belmont. Make no mistake, Jaylen had no desire to meet up with Belmont to learn more about him, but that didn't stop my best friend from asking every question in the book. Where had he come from? Why was he here? How did he know about me? Where does he get his money? Hearing Jaylen ask those questions made me realize I had the same ones myself.

The one thing I didn't do was ask about his family again. After the picture debacle, things were a little tense. It wasn't worth the risk—I needed Belmont. I guessed he missed his wife and kids, and it made me worry about my future. I'd distanced myself from my family as much as I could, but I still got to see them. I dreaded the day I'd have to walk away like he did. I understood why he didn't want to talk about it or anything personal.

Another burning question Jaylen and I had: Was there a cure? A way to somehow reverse this? I did plenty of googling on my own and came up empty—aside from the websites that insisted the only way to cure it was to *kill* me. Jaylen, on the other hand—well, turned out he was a master researcher.

"I'm just saying give it a try," he said one day.

"No." I rolled my eyes. "Where did you find this? It sounds more like a dare or trick, than a cure."

"It was on a mommy blog—don't laugh!" Jaylen couldn't contain his own laughter. "Come on, if a mom thinks her kid is a zombie, don't you think she's going to do the most thorough research?"

"No." I stared at the concoction Jaylen had mixed prior to his arrival—mayo with six kinds of essential oils, holy water, and pudding. Chocolate pudding. "I think the lady is mentally ill. Is her kid okay? She really made her baby eat it? I think we need to call CPS, man."

"Okay, okay." He held his hands up defensively. "So she doesn't exactly *have* kids, but it was a theory. She's a witch doctor. And you don't eat it, you just smear it on your skin. Something with the mayo being the carrier for it all, the oils repairing what's broken, and the holy water removing evil. Come on, you don't know what lengths I had to go through to get the holy water."

"And the pudding?" I asked.

"To keep you sweet." Jaylen smiled.

"Fine," I relented.

The brown concoction did nothing but make me smell weird—according to Jaylen—and my skin slick with grease. But hey, that didn't stop him from trying to find another cure.

Over the next few weeks, when I wasn't doing homework, looking for ways to reverse this thing, or hanging out with Jaylen watching zombie movies, I spent all my evenings with Belmont, learning how to fit in. There were simple things like how and where to spray the deodorizer for maximum benefit, or what internal organs would eventually rot away entirely, and how to part my hair to give it the most lifelike appearance. We used strong bleach on my teeth to keep them as close to natural as possible, and I had almost mastered the art of applying makeup in just the right amounts to keep it unnoticeable.

One day in homeroom, Jaylen nearly blew my cover.

"Pink? You seriously got a *pink* makeup bag?" He laughed loudly.

"It's not mine." I gritted my teeth.

"Naw, I'm just playing." Jaylen quickly tried to recover as the entire homeroom stared in my direction.

"Let me see." Shelby practically ran toward us, swiped my backpack, and yanked out the metallic pink bag. "Wow, Calvin, so pretty."

Hey, it was a gift with purchase, and it fit my stuff perfectly. What was I supposed to do?

"Ha, ha." I tried to play it cool. "Be careful with that, it's a gift."

"Oh really?" She unzipped it.

I jumped to my feet and ripped it from her hands.

"Yeah really, Shelby. It's for my girlfriend," I said. If I could feel my heart, it would be racing. "Doesn't Isaac give you presents?"

Her expression changed from smug to mad almost instantly. "Whatever." She turned to the class. "Hey, everyone, Calvin here has a girlfriend, and he buys her makeup. She must be a real ug-o, so they're perfectly matched."

"Okay, okay," Jaylen said, taking the bag back, "you made your point."

Shelby turned on her heel and returned to her desk.

"Sorry," Jaylen mouthed.

I shrugged. I couldn't be mad at him. But dang, there went my shot with having a girlfriend since, apparently, I was already taken.

***

Of all the reasons to hang out with Belmont on almost a nightly basis, him keeping me fed was the most important. I had to say, the mortuary business was booming. Samuel, the delivery boy, did his job, and made a small fortune on the side.

At first, I still had trouble getting all psyched for mealtimes. The next few bodies sent me reeling like the first two did, and only after Belmont had revealed the brains did I finally settle down. By the third week, however, the newness wore off. Since I was no longer a rookie, Belmont even allowed me to make the cuts—which was easy, given I was only cutting through sutures. I wasn't going to lie. Sawing open a dead person's head was quite a rush. Not to say I enjoyed cutting it open. It just didn't necessarily damage my conscience. People went hunting all the time, right? They'd shoot a deer and gut it right out in the open without a second's hesitation. Man . . . deer . . . okay, they weren't the same. But still, it made sense in my head.

After nearly a month, I felt the hope for a normal life on the horizon. All I had to do was stick to a short list of rules.

No doctors unless I wanted to relocate permanently to some government lab. I guess they just didn't find a walking corpse a laughable condition. No law enforcement, especially those with K-9 units, because dogs could sniff out our abnormalities from a mile away. I had to keep minimal contact and communication with my parents, which was tough on what I thought had been a good relationship. But it was better than trying to explain to them everything. I couldn't imagine what they would've done had I brought one of my sack lunches to the dinner table. Disastrous.

I figured I'd make the break away from my parents gradually. I had plenty of time as long as I kept eating.

I had to keep up on my appointments with Belmont. Embalming, latex makeup application—which took forever and felt girly—plus for the first year, I'd have to soak my hair in some funky conditioner to keep it from fraying and falling out. I spent more time in front of the bathroom mirror than ever. Belmont even gave me a sleeping bag filled with a solid form of the Abram's deodorizer to lie in every night. They were like those little packages of silicone beads you found inside a new pair of sneakers, only bigger and kind of squishy.

No alcohol or cigarettes, which hadn't been a problem before, but Belmont insisted on drilling it into my head nonetheless. Apparently, the smoke would most likely react with the formaldehyde coursing through my veins. And definitely no drugs, nothing with needles. It was okay. I would be okay. I could follow the rules.

"So I can't die?" I asked one evening in November. We had just eaten some old woman who had died of liver cancer. She had to be in her mid-eighties. Frumpy, wrinkly, and her eyes kept fluttering and flicking open during our meal. That happened from time to time. It had to do with the nerve synapses or something. Regardless, it should have weirded me out, but I found more interest in it than disgust.

"Why so interested in that, Calvin?" Belmont asked, handing me the mop. The whole room likely smelled of death—not that I'd know. We now shared all cleaning responsibilities equally, but I always asked for the mopping. Lingering around the gurney still didn't sit well with me after meals.

"I don't know. It's cool, right? We're kind of like superheroes, aren't we? I mean, we don't have any special powers and we're clumsy and all that, but nothing can hurt us." Jaylen and I had actually discussed this earlier in the day. Invincibility trumped all other powerful abilities. Except, of course, for X-ray vision.

"Yeah, superheroes." Belmont chuckled. Down on his knees, he worked the hot, soapy sponge over the legs of the gurney, removing all splattered blood and tissue. "That's the dumbest thing I've ever heard. Who would want to be saved by a zombie?"

"You know what I mean. We're invincible."

"No, we most certainly are not. And that sort of talk will get you killed."

"But you said I can't die." I ceased mopping and stared at Belmont instead of the smeared crimson mess on the ground.

"I never said that. With the proper treatment, you can live for a very long time. Two hundred, three hundred years, maybe. But decomposition will eventually take hold. Nothing lasts forever, especially if you go and do something stupid."

Together, we carried the mop bucket to the washroom sink. It was heavy and sloshy and teeming with small fragments of skull, wiry hair, and blood. There was always a surprising amount of blood.

"Stupid as in . . ."

"As in causing yourself an irreparable injury."

"I don't get it," I said. "I broke my arm and I didn't even feel it. Plus, you fixed it, so it moves fine." The wire bone mesh hidden beneath my skin really did work. My arm had absolute mobility, with no evidence of a break.

"Yes, I did."

"And let's say I get hit by a car. Inconvenient? Sure. I'd have to hobble back here for you to fix me, but I'm sure you could."

"Only if your head is still intact."

"Right . . ." I nodded, but my voice trailed off with uncertainty.

"Your brain cannot be damaged. Remember?" Belmont asked. "Your brain is the link. If you suffer a severe head injury, you will die. If your brain is crushed in a car accident or in a terrible fall, it's over." With that, he turned on the hot water and washed out the remaining residue in the bucket.

I took a moment to think about that. Severe head injury. Crushed brain. All so gruesome, but if that was the only way Belmont knew of to kill a zombie, the odds were still in my favor. Yeah, it was dramatic, but who was going to crush my brain? I didn't have enemies, so nothing like that would happen to me.

Another week went by, and Thanksgiving neared. My ties with my parents grew stressed, to say the least, but it would be virtually impossible to avoid spending a holiday meal away from them. For the past month and a half, our interactions had grown more and more distant. I never ate meals with them anymore, though I did pick up groceries to help Mom out. It was the least I could do. I ran out of the house right before school and snagged a couple of granola bars from the pantry just to keep her from raising any questions. I chucked them in the dumpster just before boarding the bus.

At lunch, I always grabbed a tray of whatever Jaylen was eating. That way, when he begged, which he always did, I had plenty of options for him to munch on at the table. The rest of my meal I nibbled on, figuring a little vomit couldn't hurt me.

My dad worked a lot of evenings, so dinner became a regular fend-for-yourself ordeal. Perfect for me. But Thanksgiving? I didn't even want to think of the aftermath I'd create in the bathroom after that meal. Unless I really wanted to raise their suspicions, I would have to eat something. Water was key in making the upchuck process a bit smoother.

On a Monday evening in mid-November, my mom hit me with disturbing news.

"Calvin," she called through my door. The clock read nine p.m., and I knew she was headed to bed. I had been lying in my sleeping bag, watching the numbers slowly advance on my alarm clock toward eleven. My meetings with Belmont were the only things I really lived for at night. That and late-night horror flicks. Or research, as I liked to call them.

The awful grind of heavy metal music pumped through my stereo, drowning out most of the sounds outside my room. Honestly, I hated it. So loud. So angry. Most of the time, I couldn't understand a word those dudes were screaming. Just banging drums and growling. I'd always considered myself a classic rock type of guy.

My room disgusted my mom. She hardly ever came in anymore. Posters of evil-looking guys with long hair and mascara covered every possible inch of my walls. I owned several stone skulls and weird crystal daggers. I had stuff that made no sense whatsoever, but managed to make my mother's skin crawl whenever she passed in the hallway and my door happened to be open.

Poor Mom. I hated torturing her. But I had to consider the alternative. I'd dust and vacuum after school tomorrow, show her that I still cared. At least, I hoped it'd make her feel like I wanted to still be a part of the family.

I heard her call out once more, and when I didn't answer at first, her voice grew louder.

"Can you turn that down for a second?" she shouted above the roar.

Finally, I complied. A few seconds later, I opened my door, but instead of entering, she remained in the hallway, her eyes drifting past me to my walls. Though she made no real indication of despising my decorations, those eyes told the truthful story. They returned and rested on me.

"Can I talk to you?" she asked. She didn't look good. Tired and haggard. Like she'd been working all day and realized more work lay in store for her that night. I wanted to hug her and tell her sorry for being such a loser, but I couldn't. Belmont had warned me. One act of kindness could erase all my hard work in an instant. It sounded like one of those inspirational quotes.

"Whatever," I replied.

"There's been a change in plans," she said. "For Thanksgiving."

"What do you mean?"

"Your grandmother, as you know, has been sick and isn't doing so well."

"Yeah, I know. So?" I was a jerk. My grandmother on my dad's side was a sweet lady who always had boxed chocolates scattered around her house and served us ginger ale and pound cake whenever we visited, which didn't happen too often. Lately, she'd been sick and even made a couple of trips to the emergency room. I knew my dad felt guilty about being away from her.

"She's requested we come visit her for the holiday. It will probably be her last one." My mom paused, sniffing the air. Probably checking for cigarette smoke, so when she didn't smell anything, she appeared satisfied. "Your father and I want you to come with us."

Visit my grandma? That was a bad idea. If Grammy had been well and that just happened to be a pleasant, surprise-type idea, then I could've easily refused or pitched a fit. Believe me, my parents didn't enjoy hanging around with someone with a sour attitude. But every day, my grandmother inched closer to dying. This was an argument I couldn't win. Plus, I really wanted to see her one last time.

So even though I gave some effort into whining and griping about the trip, about how I had other plans and my mom never considered or cared about what was going on in my life, I didn't make it too difficult for her to win the argument. In the end, I just shrugged, gave my mom a slight nod, and for a fleeting moment, I caught a smile on her face as she backed away from the iron maiden I called a bedroom.

"You'll make her very happy, son. Thank you," she

said. "We fly out in a week, on Wednesday afternoon, and we'll come home on Sunday evening."

I closed the door and dropped to my knees. Belmont was going to be ticked! Four days? We would be gone for four days! A barrage of questions entered my head. How was I supposed to go without food for four days? No, make that five days, because unless Belmont agreed to a Wednesday brunch with brains, I'd have my last meal on Tuesday night. How did zombies respond to airplanes? Did we wig out? Did the change in cabin pressure force us to attack the flight attendants? Did the hotel have good plumbing? Because I was going to destroy the bathroom. Oh, this was not good at all.

# Chapter 12

"Out of the question," Belmont said. We had just finished eating the brain of a transient man who had the mishap of falling off a cargo car of a train. His head was so severely damaged in the fall, we hadn't even been sure the brain would be edible.

I could think of no accurate way to describe flavor when dealing with brains, but there were differences. Old age had its effect. You could almost taste the staleness, like moldy cheese. The perfect meal came from someone in their mid-thirties. Male or female, it didn't matter. At that age, the brain matured like a fine wine. We ate teenager about two weeks ago. A little tough and chewy. Belmont said teenagers always came off as a waste, since they didn't really use that much of their brain. Funny, huh? Yeah, he was a real riot. I hadn't tried a child yet, nor did I plan to. I mean, I had my limits.

"I don't have much of a choice." I doused my hands with sanitizer and chucked the empty container into a garbage sack. Lately, Belmont had decided our meetings should be more spread out. If I kept coming over every night, someone was bound to find out. He had a point. Jaylen found out easily enough, and he was no Sherlock Holmes.

"You always have a choice. You just have to decide on what's more important to you. Keeping your mother and father satisfied or your hunger. Choosing one of those options might result in death."

"But don't you understand family needs?" I picked at a piece of lodged gray matter in my front teeth. "Surely you had a family. How did you explain all this to them?" Belmont hesitated with the mop bucket, and I caught a glimpse of actual sadness in his eyes. He opened his mouth to speak, but then shook it away.

This wasn't my first attempt to pry information from him. Yeah, I had started to fit back into society. I didn't stink, I always stayed well fed, and I owed all this to Belmont. Yet some things still didn't add up.

Every night, while I stared at the ceiling, I thought about how this had happened. Why was there even a Lich Stone in the mausoleum in the first place? And most importantly, I thought about Belmont. Where had he come from? Why did he just happen to show up a few days after my change? And though he looked about in his forties, I knew he had to be so much older. Plus, I wanted to know what happened to his family. I mean, he had to come from *somewhere*.

Other than an occasional comment about his former career as a neurobiologist, he kept quiet about his past. I didn't even know his last name, which I guess didn't really matter. And I still hadn't uncovered where all this money came from that he was paying Samuel, other than "old money." When it came to social talk, I did all the talking. He was one stubborn dude when it came to opening up.

Jaylen questioned this, thinking Belmont must have had some deep dark secrets he was concealing. We talked about it last weekend. Jaylen told me to keep fishing for answers, and if I saw an opening, I should strike, even though the last time I'd tried had gone terribly.

Well, Belmont had just given me a clear opening.

"You need to start talking." My words were blurted out so abruptly, they even caught me by surprise.

Belmont's head jerked up. He looked at me and then away, but I wouldn't let him get out of this to sneak back down into his hidden world.

"Where do you come from? How freaking old are you? Come on, man! I've played by the rules. I've done everything you've asked. You've got to tell me something. Anything!" I sounded desperate, but I deserved some information, didn't I?

Belmont lowered the bucket into the washroom sink and dried his hands on a towel. "The year of my turning was 1874."

He was from 1874? That was over a century ago. Impossible! But no, I knew it wasn't impossible.

The oldest people in the world couldn't even live that long, and they were shriveled up prunes. I had to be sensitive with the matter. Belmont had finally opened up, and if I didn't go easy with my words, I would offend him and he'd close back up like a clam.

"How old were you? Where did you live?" Those were fair, safe questions. At least I hoped they were.

Belmont paused, contemplating. "I was forty-three years old, and I lived in a quiet town. I had a beautiful wife and two young daughters."

*The picture!*

"We farmed. Mostly livestock. Sheep. We had an orchard with over two hundred Jonathan apple trees. It was a good life until Hester, my wife, contracted tuberculosis." Belmont's eyes glazed. Not with tears, but a definite change overcame them as nostalgia kicked in.

"I did all I could to help her," he whispered, his voice strained. "Called in the best doctors in the neighboring communities. Tried all sorts of medicines. But the illness had taken too strong a hold on her body. It was a dangerous disease, and no one knew how to contain it. The mayor issued a strict quarantine of our property, and all interaction with doctors and neighbors was forbidden. It was a death sentence for her, and perhaps for our whole family if the illness spread. We were told to stay put until Hester passed away and enough time went by to conclude the rest of my family was either going to die as well or recover."

Belmont stared at me, his eyes large and haunting. His voice grew ragged. "She was fading. My sweet Hester was dying right in front of me. In my desperation, I ventured down a dark path. A stranger came to our home one evening. We spoke on the porch, and I knew immediately something was different about him. Yet he spoke of a cure. Of a solution for Hester and my family. What else could I do? If I didn't try, I would live with the regret of not knowing.

"He led me to a church that night. Not a church of worship, but of something else. Something dark, thick with evil. It was there where he introduced me to the practice of necromancy and the use of a Lich Stone. Something had caught hold of his soul, and he was looking for victims. I was his first. I don't remember much about the transformation. It happened so fast and so unexpectedly, I was unaware of any change to my body."

All other sounds in the room vanished. It was as though my mind had taken me back to the 1800s on

Belmont's farm. As he recounted the horrors of his disease, I could see everything as though I stood there in the farmhouse. I remembered the image I'd briefly seen of Belmont's wife and children while he supplied the story material.

"At first, I thought I had finally succumbed to tuberculosis, as nothing would appease my hunger. My days were spent vomiting. I was taken to sudden fits of anger. My children were afraid, and Hester, poor Hester, knew. She *knew*. Maybe it was because she was so stricken and close to death herself. She was able to detect the awful change in me. I had no way of knowing how to take care of myself. To feed. To appease the hunger that grew stronger and stronger. Days passed, then a week and then . . . blackness. If only I had stayed in the blackness. I would give anything to never have another thought, another memory, to have died and vanished into nothing. They were so young, so innocent. My wife, I'm sure, felt very little, but the children . . ."

I had heard enough. I saw it in my head. Belmont, crazed and frenzied, tearing at his wife's flesh. The girls, terrified, huddled in a corner with their eyes squeezed shut and palms pressed into their ears to drown out the noise. That was enough for me. I held up a hand to stop him, and Belmont gave no further explanation. His jaw tightened and his lips pursed together.

He'd killed his own family. It was horrific, yet as gruesome as it sounded, I felt sorry for him. It was beyond his control. I didn't want to think about it anymore. To think about him when he finally came to the realization of what he had done.

"I was hanged for my crime and buried, but not with my family. Fearing my evil deed would bring about some hideous curse to the town, they buried them elsewhere in a hidden grave. At that point, even after I dangled from the noose, I knew what I had become and that I couldn't die so easily. Instead, I pretended to be dead. It was in a time when medical technology was so limited that doctors had no proper means of testing my vitals. They buried me, and my name was removed from the court records. I no longer existed."

"I'm so sorry," I said.

He continued. "I didn't wait long to claw through the fresh soil of my recently dug grave. I emerged from there with an insatiable hunger. Then I fed. I had to. I didn't know what else to do. My appetite took over and all rational thinking was gone for a time. When my hunger was satisfied and some semblance of rational thinking returned, I realized what I had done and that I had to leave. I had to hide."

"So you left," I whispered.

Belmont nodded.

"I shouldn't have bothered you about it." I actually felt embarrassed. Why had I been so pushy?

"It was good to tell you, and you deserve to know."

I knew Belmont needed to get that off his chest. He needed a friend, and maybe I could be the one to help him. We were in this together, and in a way, though it seemed totally odd, he needed me just as much as I needed him. After sharing that memory with Belmont, I felt I could get through anything with my condition. There were no problems I couldn't tackle. Not with his support.

But the following evening when I awoke in my bed, covered in blood, I knew I had made a terrible mistake.

# Chapter 13

Just after midnight, I had been in my room fully clothed except for my shoes and socks, because I had learned an embarrassing lesson after spending the evening with Belmont outside in my underwear. I had gone without sleep for quite some time and had gotten used to the idea of staying awake.

Without any warning, no dizziness or disorientation, I blacked out. One moment, I was lying down looking at the ceiling, the next moment everything was gone. When I came to, I was no longer in my room or my house. I stood inside the Crenshaw Mausoleum facing the strange stone I had seen before, and thick mist, like a fog of dry ice, swirled around at the base.

I had to be dreaming, because logically, I couldn't just appear in the cemetery. That defied all laws of physics. And if I was dreaming, I had made some serious progress. Despite the bizarreness of it all, I had to be sleeping in order to dream, and that meant maybe my body had begun to mend.

Something moved in the room with me. I felt its presence close, perhaps within reach. Footsteps, slow and deep, like the sound of heavy boots, continued until they stopped right behind me. I stood frozen in place, rooted to the floor, my fingers opening and closing in some sort of nervous impulse. The intruder breathed in my ears. No, not breathing. Whispering.

The symbols on the stone began to move, transforming into different shapes. I watched them, mystified by the transformation as the whispering continued, growing louder, more forceful. What were the words? What were they saying? It sounded garbled and incoherent, yet it registered in my subconscious. My heart pounded and rage roared in my chest. I felt something in my hands, some sort of container. I looked down at the object as my fingers pierced through the thick layer of plastic and a dark red substance oozed from it, filling my hands.

Blood.

Dripping from a plastic donor bag. But why was I holding it?

Everything dimmed, and then more blackness surrounded me.

My eyes snapped open, and I found myself back in my room, lying on my bed.

"What a nightmare." I groaned, rubbing my face with my hands, and smearing something wet all over my chin. Had I been drooling? I peered at the dark substance staining my fingers. It was far thicker and darker than saliva.

"No," I whispered. I flicked on the lamp and discovered blood on my hands and all over my shirt. My feet were wet as well. A damp sludge—a mixture of mud, leaves, and grass—was smeared across my toes. Swinging my muddy feet to the side, I stumbled off the bed.

I wandered down the hall and into the bathroom. The image staring back from the mirror horrified me. I looked like the victim of a slasher movie. Blood covered my chin. Drops of it had splattered on my cheeks and forehead. And my hands were absolutely dredged in the stuff. Fear caught hold of me in the worst way. Whimpering, I tore off my clothes and searched my body for the wounds. Where were they? They had to be massive. I was lucky to be alive with how much blood I had lost. Maybe I clipped an artery. Had I fallen somewhere in the cemetery? Did I still have blood?

I swallowed dryly.

The cemetery?

But that was just a dream. How could I have been in the cemetery? There was no physical way. Hudson Cemetery was ten miles across town. Even if I could've taken one of my parents' cars without them knowing, how would I have driven it while I was unconscious?

The mausoleum had felt real, and all the evidence seemed to pile up against me. I saw the dirt on my feet from walking through the freshly watered cemetery grounds. Beneath the layer of blood on my palms, I could see tattered flesh, and a fleeting image of scaling the cemetery gate entered my mind. If that was true and my mind recalled things correctly, then where had all this blood come from?

Then I remembered the dream. Someone had placed a blood donor bag in my hands, and I had ripped it open. I rested my stained fingers on the edge of the sink and stared once again at my reflection, entertaining a new, frightening possibility. If it hadn't been a dream, then I really did go to the cemetery all by myself. I walked there. And if that was true, then that blood soaking my hands and shirt and chin wasn't mine.

***

The next morning, the headlines blared all over the news.

Massacre!

A loving husband ripped from his family at the hands of a cruel killer. Every channel played and replayed the images of a Victorian-style home with creeping vines on the walls, and police caution tape surrounding the property. Neighbors gathered by the driveway, clinging to each other, most of them sobbing or in a state of disbelief. The words flashed across the screen. A religious man, murdered. The body was found in a closet. Blood everywhere, and the worst, most unthinkable death. Decapitation. The dead man's family was inconsolable. How could such an important individual in the community have been so brutally murdered? The Reverend S. Maxwell Grossier was dead.

And I had killed him.

I knew it. Yeah, there was no definite proof—yet. I didn't have time to run DNA checks on the blood that night to match it with the reverend while I was busy stripping off my clothes and piling them in a garbage sack to be burned before dawn. But it had to be me. Somehow, I had killed him.

Wait, that was crazy talk! But I seemed to be all about crazy talk now.

Something inside me told me the blood from my dream, vision, or whatever you wanted to call it, had come from Reverend Grossier. Maybe it was my conscience. Yeah, that could be it. Jiminy Cricket told me the truth, of all things. Only Jiminy was a zombie cricket.

I didn't even know the man. He lived in Jefferson. I didn't attend his congregation. We didn't share a relative. He didn't have any kids my age that I would've bumped into at a baseball game. And yet, I had killed him.

But why?

My insides felt like a head-on collision while I watched the news. I kept peering over my shoulder, expecting the door to break down and the officers in blue to appear with guns blazing.

"Can you believe this, John?" I heard my mother ask my dad from behind me on the couch. "It's like a horror movie."

I shuddered, not from the repeating scenes on the television screen, but from my mother's words. She was so disgusted. Well, of course she was disgusted. Normal people would find decapitation disgusting.

What would my parents do when they found out? And they would find out. Judging by the amount of blood I discovered covering my body last night, I wasn't exactly careful concealing the evidence. The feds were going to find my fingerprints, or some hair or spit or something, and it would lead them right to my house. My dad would kill me! And not in just the hypothetical sense. Okay, maybe I was thinking irrationally. He probably wouldn't kill me, but I could guarantee he'd never come and visit me once I'd been locked up behind bars.

In prison! Or worse, some government lab.

I couldn't go to prison. Prison was for criminals. Hardened criminals. Criminals with no future and with vendettas. They'd go nuts on a kid like me. And what would happen when I'd been there for over a week? Who would I eat? A guard? The warden? My cellmate?

Literally, those were the thoughts racing through my mind as I sat and listened to my parents carry on about the atrocities happening so close to home. I needed to see Belmont, and it couldn't wait until nightfall.

I shot up from the floor, knocking into the coffee table.

"Where are you off to?" my mom asked as I snagged my coat and beelined for the garage.

"To Jaylen's," I lied. It was Saturday, and I shouldn't really need a reason to ride my bike to my best friend's house. I probably could've asked for the car keys, but I didn't want to have any further conversation, nor did I necessarily want to be on the road in my parents' Suburban, being chased by cop cars. A bike was safe, and if the unthinkable happened, the police could take me down quickly without much fuss. The last thing I needed was to have my arrest broadcast live on the news while Mommy and Daddy watched from the living room.

"Okay, but I want you home before dark." My mother stood, folding her arms. "You are not to be out, even to the movies, until they catch this creep and lock him up."

I wanted to run over and give my mom a goodbye hug. Heck, I'd even give one to Dad, but I couldn't bring myself to do it. I'd find some other indirect way to help out around the house. It was all I could do.

This sucked.

# Chapter 14

Belmont sat cross-legged on his mattress, his face blank and expressionless. I told him everything, at least what I could remember, from the night before. I told him of the unexpected sleep and waking in the mausoleum. I told him of the stone and the moving symbols and the whispering voice in my ear. I still remembered the strange warmth my body felt in the tomb. I didn't know how I got there. I remembered the owner of the voice standing close to me as I received instructions, but I couldn't remember what he told me. It had been garbled gibberish. Yet in my mind, and at the time, I understood.

When I finished, Belmont gnawed on the end of a pencil. Manuals and big, thick books without covers and barely any bindings, surrounded him on the floor and hung off the edge of the mattress. Since he normally didn't venture out of his home until after dark, he had neglected to apply any makeup. Gaunt and gray, his skin bore the true semblance of a walking corpse.

Belmont uncrossed his legs and placed his hands

behind his head. "Interesting," he finally sniffed after several moments of contemplation.

"You believe me, then?" I asked. I guess it would've suited me better if he had been in more denial and had said something like, "You're blowing things out of proportion. Wait until we have all of the facts," but I didn't need the facts. My gut and my mind knew the truth. The sooner everyone accepted this, the better.

He nodded, his expression sad and almost apologetic. "I was afraid this could happen to you."

"What's happening to me?" I clapped my hands to the side of my face and dug my fingers through my fake hair. Admittedly, it was nice to be able to do this without uprooting any strands, but I found no pleasure in it at the moment.

"You've been summoned." Belmont stood and bent over a tower of books.

"Summoned?"

"Yes, Calvin, summoned. By a necromancer."

"A necromancer?" I asked. The word sounded vaguely familiar, like something from a video game, but I had no clue what it meant.

"A dark sorcerer. One that uses their powers to communicate with the dead and to control them." Belmont discovered what he'd been searching for, thumbed through to the right page, and offered me the book.

The page had been previously dog-eared. It was an illustration of a Lich Stone, a large one with foreign black markings. Surrounding the stone were gray rock walls, dripping with murky water from the ceiling. The artist depicted the stone as glowing radiantly, and standing in front of the stone was a zombie.

Déjà vu.

It hit me like a punch to the face. This could be a

picture of me. The zombie looked older and wore what looked like farmer's clothing—overalls, boots, a bandana around his neck—but the surroundings resonated an eerie familiarity. The image of someone standing behind the zombie in a dark red cloak caused me the greatest amount of uneasiness. The hood blocked all visibility of the person's face, but his hand rested on the zombie's shoulder, and he appeared to be in the process of whispering something into his ear.

"This is a summoning ritual. The necromancer has gained control of the Lich Stone, and with it has also gained the will of the zombie. Once the ritual has been completed, the zombie will do whatever it is instructed to do. In most cases, it involves the murder of some enemy of the necromancer. This dark sorcery has been around for ages." Belmont tapped the image of the Lich Stone in the picture. "Such a Lich Stone can be found in the mausoleum you entered, and now we must focus on the matter at hand. You've been summoned and thus have committed murder." Belmont approached me and placed his hands on my shoulders.

"I've been summoned by a necromancer. Like the one that turned you into a zombie? Is he the one doing this?" Maybe that wasn't a rational question, but who had time for rational questions anymore?

Belmont smiled. "No, no. That man has long since died. I saw to that myself."

"Then who's doing this?" I asked. Just when I thought things had returned to a state of normalcy, something new had come along to crush it like a skull.

"It could be anyone, but more than likely, it is someone with a history of dark practices."

"Well, that narrows it down, doesn't it?" I couldn't

help but be sarcastic. "Did you know this would happen to me?"

Belmont lowered his eyes. "I didn't know for sure."

"But you had an idea," I pressed.

He sighed.

"Unbelievable! Now, here I am, no doubt headed to life in prison with the blood of an innocent preacher on my hands, and maybe, just maybe, I could've done something to prevent this."

"Calvin, you don't understand. It's not that simple."

"Oh, but it is. You knew I was going to go off killing people, and yet you did nothing to stop it or even warn me." I hauled off and booted a stack of papers, sending them flying around the room like a swarm of kites.

"Just listen to me and I'll explain," Belmont started, but I had gone too far to just surrender now.

"My life's over. My family's going to disown me. Maybe I'm not religious, but I kind of believe in heaven and I'm sure murderers don't get ushered in too often. So where am I headed?"

"They don't know who did it yet," Belmont interjected. "And chances are they never will. Our bodies don't leave evidence. Our DNA is not matched in any databases, nor are our fingerprints traceable. You destroyed your clothing. You burned it, right?" I pawed at my eyes in frustration but managed a nod. "Good. You did the right thing. This crime happened in Jefferson. Yes, it's close and the investigation will spill into our neighborhoods, but we can keep you hidden until . . ." He hesitated.

"Until what?" I shouted.

"Until it happens again."

"What do you mean happens again?" I paced the small room.

"Make no mistake, they *will* call again."

"Fine, then I'll start handcuffing myself to the bed."

"Do you value your hand?" Belmont sighed. "You will be powerless to resist the summoning. If that means dragging your entire bed, or ripping off your own hand, you'll do it if that means getting to the necromancer."

"Then I'll start hiding in my dad's gun case. It has like the biggest locks you've ever seen." I shook my head. "There has to be a way."

"I cannot stress enough what a terrible idea that is." Belmont slumped further. "You'll just keep walking into the walls of it, likely damaging your head and brain. I'm sorry, Calvin. You need to accept your reality."

A gong sounded in my head, and it tolled a note of finality. The Reverend Grossier's death wouldn't be my last kill.

# Chapter 15

Human hair.

I found human hair clutched in my hands when I awoke two nights later in my bedroom. Not a strand. Not several strands. A thick clump. It had only been two nights since the Reverend Grossier's murder. The yellow police tape hadn't even been removed, the investigation still ongoing. And now this.

There was mud and blood covering me too. On my neck and shoulders. My shirt wasn't as soaked as it had been with the reverend's blood, but I found a copious amount of mud saturating it. Quietly, I stood from my bed and undressed out of the soiled clothing. I crept downstairs and returned to my room with two garbage bags.

I dumped everything. My sheets, my pillowcases, a pair of old jeans I had worn the day before but had left on the floor next to my hamper. I had to dispose of all of it. Those were Belmont's instructions. Though he promised I wouldn't leave evidence behind at the crime scene, any blood-covered articles would be a dead giveaway. Dogs were trained to sniff out a trail. Thus, I'd have to burn everything to remove the scent. I filled a trash bag with my offending clothes and dropped the hair in last. It fell in a clump, resting atop the filthy clothes. Long and black.

The hair of a woman.

After two days and two crimes, I had already developed a regular routine of concealing my dirty deeds.

I snuck out of the house and rode my bike to Belmont's. Together, we destroyed the evidence behind the meat-processing factory. The fire blazed bright and tall, and the plastic garbage bags produced a plume of green smoke in the night sky. We stood next to each other, watching it burn in silence.

An hour passed, the flames leaving nothing but the smoldering remains of my blue jeans. Belmont poked at the ashes with a stick and then poured a bucket of cold water over the pit, extinguishing the fire almost completely.

Afterward, we entered his room and sat across from each other on the mattress. Newer books had joined the ranks of his previous collection. A few were open to various chapters containing information on necromancy and other sadistic rituals.

"This has to stop," I muttered.

"I agree," Belmont answered. "The necromancer's powers are growing. And with that, so does his confidence."

"You're assuming it's a *he,* then," I said.

Belmont shrugged. "I'm assuming, yes, but it could be a female, I suppose."

I looked down at my hands, now scrubbed clean, but before . . . red and bloody. I shook my head. "No, it's a man. I know it." I could remember the voice whispering instruction into my eager ears. Not a female. Definitely a man. I wanted so badly to cry and to show true emotion. Something. Some sort of remorse for the horrific deeds I had done. I couldn't just kill people. It wasn't in my nature. I had morals, and killing was wrong! This necromancer proved determined to turn me into something hideous.

"What do you remember?" Belmont asked. "From tonight, what do you remember?"

I closed my eyes and the memories formed. I allowed myself to immerse completely, which took me back a few hours to when it had happened.

"It started like the other time. I was knocked unconscious somehow, and then woke up in the mausoleum. Everything was like before. The stone, the symbols, all of it very similar. And again, like the time before, I heard someone whispering in my ear."

"That would be the necromancer," Belmont said softly.

I nodded. "I remember him placing something in my hand—something feathery and light. My fingers closed around it, but I don't remember what he gave me. That part seems vague."

"Don't worry about that just yet. Go on."

I paused to breathe deeply and jumped when the lights from a car out on the road flashed by, temporarily illuminating Belmont's dark lodgings.

"I walked a great distance," I continued, surprised by how much more I could remember this time. "I clung to the shadows in the surrounding forest because something was telling me I had to. Like some subliminal instructions to stay hidden. Then I arrived at a park."

"Do you remember which one? Ludlow? Iverson Memorial?" Belmont asked, interrupting my train of thought.

"No, neither one of those. I did see statues, though. One of a man playing Frisbee with a dog and another one, more obscure, not in my immediate line of sight. There were several park benches surrounding a fountain, but I think the water had been turned off. That's when I saw her. She was sitting on one of the benches. I couldn't see her face, just the back of her head and her black hair. She had her hands in her lap, and I can still see her feet fidgeting beneath the bench. She was wearing heels and um . . ." I snapped my fingers. "She had a string of pearls around her neck. I don't know for sure, but I think she was waiting for someone. Like a date or something like that. But there didn't seem to be anyone else around."

"You're sure of this?" Belmont asked. He plucked a pencil from the desk and rolled it between his thumb and forefinger.

"Yeah, I mean I think."

"You didn't see anyone else there?" he pressed.

I hesitated, realizing the importance of this part of the story. Had there been other people in the park when I attacked, there would be more witnesses. More people who would've seen me and what I had done. I closed my eyes, willing my memory to clear up, and then shook my head. "I'm positive we were alone."

Belmont stared at me, absentmindedly rolling the pencil. "Let's hope."

"Anyway, I came up on the woman from behind. I was fast and calculated. When I was practically on top of her, she turned and saw me. Her face lit up at first, probably expecting whomever it was she had been waiting for, but then she took on a different expression. She looked surprised, then confused, and then . . . horrified. She was so pretty, and she had beautiful hair," I said. "Kind of short but stylish. Like barely shoulder—" I stopped mid-sentence.

"What is it?"

"Um, nothing, I guess." My memory felt all screwy. How could she have had short hair? The hair in my hand had been long and flowing, like the remains of a ponytail. But hers had been different. "I think I'm confused."

"Can you continue?" Belmont asked.

"I can remember. I heard her scream. She tried to run, but she was no match for my speed, and I jumped on her. I attacked so quickly, yanking away her hands as she struggled. I remember honing my fingers in on her throat and closing them around her skin." I stopped and looked at Belmont, my mind distorting. Things grew hazy from this point on in my memory. Maybe that was due to how dark the park had been.

"Go on," Belmont prodded. "What happened next?" He had dropped the pencil on the bed and now sat up, eagerly awaiting the conclusion of my awful story.

I blinked several times, my eyes narrowing. "I . . . I . . . don't remember, really. I think I must've blacked out for a moment. Because I can remember opening my eyes and seeing her crumpled over the barrier of the fountain. But I was far away from her at that point. Like a good twenty feet."

"Is it possible you had finished the job and then started back to your home?" Belmont asked.

I didn't answer immediately. There was something odd about the ending of the memory. Something different. I didn't remember killing her. Maybe that was a good thing. Memories of murdering a woman, or anyone for that matter, would probably haunt me for the rest of my existence. Maybe I had gotten lucky and had blacked out during the most grueling parts.

"Yeah," I finally said. "Yeah, maybe that's it. I must've dragged her into the fountain and tried to leave. But then I don't remember anything else until I opened my eyes and I was back in my bedroom."

The mood in the room had grown solemn and depressing. Like we were the last two participants in a group therapy session to share our troubled pasts.

"How can I stop this?" I asked, my hands trembling. I didn't feel temperature. Nothing cold. But the memory of that poor woman dying by my hands sent terrible shakes through my fingertips.

"You have to find the necromancer and put an end to it," Belmont said, his voice low.

"But he could be anywhere." These crimes weren't happening in Jewkes. I had been everywhere in this town, and I would've remembered that park. If they were happening in Jefferson, then there were thousands of possibilities. My search could go on for years without results.

I gazed around the room, finally resting on the piles of newspapers next to the mattress. They were recent, and the first two or three were spread out, revealing their origins. The *Jewkes Daily Tribune,* the *Lindonville Herald,* and the *Chidester Sun.* Belmont had a particular interest in the news from the local cities. On the floor spread out by the nightstand, the front page of the *Jefferson Gazette* from two days ago lay folded over. On it, the headline read, "Beloved Minister Murdered." Belmont had highlighted some of the words and names in the article.

"The good news is that we know the location of the Lich Stone, which means he or she has to be close," Belmont said. "It's not much of a lead, but it's better than nothing."

"You're right!" I turned away from the papers. The Lich Stone! Of course. That was a definite lead. "The

Crenshaw Mausoleum. This necromancer has been there, inside with me. Maybe he's left a trail or clues by mistake." I walked over to the window and climbed the first few steps of the ladder. "We need to go there now while it's still fresh. Maybe he hasn't left yet!" It was the best idea I'd had in quite a while. Maybe, with proper investigation, we could find out about the necromancer and stop the killing.

Belmont hadn't risen from his bed. Couldn't he see the urgency?

"Are you coming?" I asked.

His eyes appeared sympathetic. Did he think I was being unreasonable? Well, excuse me for getting a little excited to put an end to my murderous rampage. So I was a little gung-ho to take off after someone in possession of dark sorcery. Okay, yeah, come to think of it, I was being a little rash. How was I supposed to square off with a necromancer? Were there things I needed to know? Spells? Weapons? I had no clue, but Belmont sure did a lot of studying on it, and together we could take him. I felt certain of it.

"I can't go there, Calvin." Belmont's voice hovered above a whisper.

"Why not?" I took a step back down the ladder.

Belmont looked down at his books and then to his newspapers. "I just can't right now."

"I can't do this alone! Don't you want to help me?"

Belmont held out his hands to me. "Of course I do. And I will help, but I just . . . I just can't go there. Not now." There were his eyes again. Darting away from me, avoiding mine. What was he covering up?

I hopped down from the windowsill. "You're all talk, aren't you? This person is ruining my life! He took away my future and any hopes I have of being normal. And now he's killing people, and I'm his weapon."

"I know," Belmont said.

"Yeah, maybe you don't. Because if you really did, I think you'd help me."

Belmont licked his lips, and his eyes slowed their darting movement. "I don't know why, but I can't go there because of the Lich Stone."

I was within milliseconds of shouting, but that actually made sense. "So I guess it's just me who gets to do all the terrible things, then, eh?"

"I didn't mean it like that. I can still help you. And tomorrow night, I'll go with you to the cemetery. I won't go with you into the mausoleum, but perhaps I can help from above, on ground level." Belmont clasped his hands.

"Why not now?"

He pointed to the alarm clock on his nightstand. "It's four a.m. You need to get home, and we need to lay low while the news settles of this latest murder. Go to school. Act normal. And then tomorrow night, meet me here at eleven. After we've eaten, we'll go together to the cemetery."

I wasn't hungry. And why wasn't I hungry? I had just murdered some poor, beautiful woman. What if she had kids? Who was she waiting for in the park? That wasn't my business. Just because I murdered someone, it didn't give me the right to pass judgment on their actions. Good grief! A zombie with a conscience. Not a good combination.

I didn't want to wait another day and to leave open the possibility of yet another murder. But Belmont was right. My parents couldn't find out about my late-night dealings. They would put an end to it. Perhaps it would raise dangerous suspicions. Maybe even draw the attention of the authorities. How would I eat? What would happen to my regular embalming?

I could wait one more day. And then we would start ourselves a little witch hunt.

# Chapter 16

Riding the school bus bothered me. Maybe if the bus had been filled with just sophomores like myself, I could learn to cope with it. But no, there were freshmen and annoying juniors and seniors. They traveled in packs and gabbed about who knows what? I assumed it had to be about sports, or maybe their lack of girlfriends. It made me feel like a loser just by mere association. The only good thing about my bus route? It passed by Jaylen's house, and he had the same misfortune as me of not having a personal mode of transportation.

I watched as Jaylen hurdled over an upside-down wheelbarrow, which had been left out over the weekend, probably from his dad's failed attempt at yard work on Saturday. He boarded the bus and plopped down in the seat next to mine. We always sat near the front, which generally was reserved for goody-two-shoes. That obviously wasn't us; we wanted the quickest exit once the bus arrived at Werner High.

"What up?" Jaylen grunted. Under his armpit as usual was his baseball mitt. He glanced sideways at the seat

next to us. Sitting crammed together were three freshmen, ogling some comic book and giggling with hushed
voices. I wondered if they purchased that from the comic
book shop across from the Cobalt. What did it matter?
Jaylen shook his head in disgust but didn't say anything.

"What do you think about all this killing?" he asked,
looking at me sideways. We hadn't spoken since Friday
after school.

I had been waiting to hear his opinion. Both murders
happened over the weekend. This was our first opportunity to discuss it. This morning at breakfast, the net-
work news had been interrupted to announce the horrific
tragedy. My mother dropped a glass that shattered all
over the kitchen floor, and I had to help her clean it up.
She even started to cry when they flashed the images of
Naomi Dansbury, the woman I had murdered, wearing a
pleasant smile and a graduation cap and gown.

She was the wife of some history professor named
Garrett. Next, Channel 8 News had flashed an image of
Garrett and Naomi walking hand in hand along the bank
of a riverbed. Garrett, a squirrelly looking guy who was a
little thin and balding, had scored with his wife. She was
way out of his league. Due to the recent tragic circumstances, he wasn't readily available for an interview. Who
could blame him? Naomi's grisly remains had been discovered in Casper Park, on the southern side of Jefferson,
just west of the freeway.

Casper Park. Nope, I had never been there before last
night.

"Crazy, huh?" I asked, awkwardly. I didn't really
know what to say about it. If I said too much, would
people start to suspect me as the killer? If I said too
little, would they do the same? It was obviously mad-

ness. I fidgeted with the zipper on my backpack. "Can you believe two people were killed so close to our town?"

Jaylen raised his eyebrows. "Two? Try four."

I nodded, but then shook my head, not comprehending. "What do you mean four?" Were we not talking about the same thing?

"Don't you listen? There have been four murders in the past couple of months, and they're saying the murders have all been linked to one dude. Some whack job who's killing people for fun. Sometimes taking their heads." Jaylen slugged the back of the seat in front of us. A kid with floppy hair and dark-rimmed glasses turned to protest, but quickly changed his mind when he saw Jaylen sitting behind him.

Four? That wasn't right, was it? "Who were the others?" I asked.

"One of them was a homeless dude. It took the police a couple of weeks to ID him. That's why he didn't show up on the news until now. They figured he'd been dead for two or three months. Found him at the dump in Chidester, crumpled up with the garbage."

"Maybe he's not from the same guy." A homeless person? Not that I discriminated when I killed people, but why would I be summoned to kill transients? The timeframe made very little sense as well. I had been a zombie for about a month and a half. Any killings before that hadn't been my fault.

"It was him. Decapitated. I mean, it better be him. I don't want to think that there's more than one psycho running around." Jaylen started pounding on his mitt, working the leather with his fist and folding the fingers on top of each other to give it a nice, loose condition.

I scratched my chin, contemplating. The reverend.

Naomi. Some homeless dude. This thing had gone serial, and the bodies were piling up.

"What about the other one?" I asked. Was it another transient? Some random individual in Jefferson?

"Colby Martinson," Jaylen said with a grunt.

"Who?" My voice rose with agitation.

"Some young minister in Jefferson. He was killed Saturday night, but the police didn't discover his body until early this morning. Same story with his head, though." The bus slowed and more kids piled on. Everyone seemed solemn—everyone except for the dorks sitting next to us. So many snorts and giggles. Jaylen had apparently heard enough, and glared at the trio in agitation. They quickly slapped the comic shut and stared out the window.

I just sat there processing. Another minister. Why did I have a habit of killing religious people? That couldn't be good. Next, I thought of the dates of the murders, the one transient from more than two months ago and then the minister on Saturday night. I couldn't remember them. I looked at Jaylen and decided I needed his help. Leaning in close, I took a chance.

"Jaylen, if you could find out about the murderer, would you do something?" I whispered.

He flinched. "Of course. Wouldn't you?"

"I think I might have a lead, but it's a weird one."

"How do you figure?" Jaylen lowered his voice.

"It has to do with my condition."

His jaw dropped. Not wide open like you saw in cartoons, but it definitely slackened. It had just occurred to me he might have temporarily forgotten his best friend had become a zombie.

"You mean . . ."

"No, no," I quickly interrupted. I didn't need to start confessing to the murders of four people just yet. It was all about timing. These things needed to be handled delicately. First, I had to find and put a stop to the necromancer, and in doing that, I could use Jaylen's help. "But it could have something to do with my . . ." I looked back over my shoulder to make sure no losers behind me listened in. ". . . turning."

Jaylen chewed on his lip. His eyes narrowed. "How good a lead do you have?"

"Pretty good," I said, puffing out my cheeks. "Belmont and I are going to try and find out more tonight at the Hudson Cemetery. Do you want to come with us?"

Jaylen's eyes widened with apprehension.

"Think about it, man," I coaxed. "If you find the murderer and stop him, you'll be famous."

Jaylen's eyebrows twitched as his lower lip turned down in thought. "What about you? Don't you want to be famous?"

"Do I really need any more attention at this point in my life?" I asked with a grin. "Video cameras and high-definition televisions have a way of revealing too much, if you know what I mean."

Jaylen clicked his tongue. "True that. When are you going?"

"Midnight. You can meet us at the back gates of the cemetery, if you'd like."

The bus pulled up to the school unloading area, and everyone stood to get off. As the two of us stepped down, Jaylen slugged me in the shoulder.

"I'm in," he said.

***

Everyone at school moved around each other in discomfited silence. The teachers, the jocks, the cheerleaders, the punks, Jaylen, me . . . all of us. No one wanted to act normal. Where were the random scuffles in the hallways? Where were the loud, obnoxious catcalls from the football players whenever Jessica Madsen or Candace Everingham passed by? Or even the hall monitors and the assistant principal, who always handed out detention and basically lived to punish us? That had all stopped. A killer on the loose had changed things for everyone.

Dinner that night at eleven wasn't pleasant. Samuel delivered another blue hair. Some seventy-five-year-old man with a tiny head who died of congestive heart failure. I hardly considered the small, shriveled brain a real meal, more like an appetizer, but beggars can't be choosers.

After eating, I asked Belmont if he knew about the other murders while we started in on the cleanup. He didn't say much. He just kept to himself as he mopped, listening as I did all the talking, with zero answers to my questions. No responses from him when I questioned the dates of the murders. Wasn't that a legitimate question? Shouldn't we both be concerned about who I had been killing?

The axe dropped figuratively when I told him about Jaylen.

"Are you a complete moron?" Belmont smacked the mop handle against the wall.

That seemed a bit harsh. "Because I wanted some more help?" I asked.

"Out of the question."

"Wouldn't three pairs of eyes be better than two? Besides, Jaylen's pretty good at this whole investigative crap."

"From what I've heard about Jaylen, he has a difficult

enough time going to a public restroom without peeing on the mirrors."

I laughed. That wasn't fair, but it was funny.

Belmont didn't seem to share the humor. "He can't come."

"I already invited him," I said, feeling a little mad at myself for not clearing it with Belmont first. I guess I didn't think he would be so set against the extra company. "Jaylen's going to meet us at the cemetery at midnight. I can't just call and cancel. He really wants to help."

"Then you would chance putting his life in danger?" Belmont asked. We had cleaned the room and covered the body. All that was left to do was to turn out the lights and head out. We had about thirty minutes to arrive at the cemetery, and we were wasting it arguing next to a corpse.

"How will we put his life in danger? There will be three of us there, not to mention that two of us are already undead zombies. Surely, we could get the jump on one necromancer." Maybe I believed that, maybe I didn't. The jury was still split on that verdict, but I had warmed up to the idea of Jaylen joining us, and I wasn't ready to back down.

"In a perfect scenario, the three of us could easily overtake one man. Make no mistake, his necromantic ability changes things. He could be weak and small. He could possess no real strength or own any dangerous weapons. But the mere fact that he can control the Lich Stone puts him on a different level. He can control *us*." Belmont patted his chest emphatically. "Bend our wills. He's already made you kill. Do you want to put Jaylen in a situation like that?"

Belmont had all the answers when he felt willing to offer them. "I can't call him," I said, heaving a sigh as I realized the gravity of my mistake. "By now, he's already snuck out of his house."

Belmont growled in frustration. I had a sick feeling that he might try canceling the entire operation. But waiting any longer increased my chances of taking another life. We couldn't put this off, and I was willing to abandon Belmont altogether and go at it alone, if it came to that. Jaylen and I would be attacking blind, with no experience, but I couldn't risk the chance of killing again.

"So be it," Belmont hissed. "But we do things my way. No exceptions."

"Got it!" I agreed, feeling relieved.

Belmont growled again. "You just make sure Jaylen gets it as well."

# Chapter 17

When we arrived at the Hudson Cemetery, I began to realize how terrifying an encounter with the necromancer could be. This . . . person who got off on controlling people. Commanding murder. Anyone who could be so cavalier with life and death wasn't someone to mess with.

We parked along the side of the road by the rear entrance, in almost the exact location where I had parked the Suburban that fateful night back in October. I was scared. Scared about what we would find. Scared I would somehow come under the necromancer's power here and go off killing again. Maybe even kill Jaylen.

Then Jaylen almost got himself killed when he hopped out from behind a bush and rapped on the window with his knuckles, causing both Belmont and me to scream out. Belmont snarled, reaching for the door latch and nearly charging out of the car to attack. Jaylen just fell over laughing, oblivious to how close he had come to being impaled on one of the exterior fence posts. For having just poured out my guts to Belmont, trying to convince him how much we needed Jaylen's help, my best friend was doing a poor job in living up to the hype.

"I couldn't resist," he apologized, climbing into the back seat of the car.

Belmont whirled around, enraged. "Now, you listen to me. I will not let you put our lives in danger."

Jaylen held up his hands, shielding himself from Belmont's verbal tirade. "You got it. Won't happen again."

"How did you get here?" I asked, feeling the need to ease the tension. Jaylen didn't have his license yet, and riding a bike to the cemetery would take all night.

A goofy grin stretched across his face. "I caught my sister making out with her boyfriend last week in my dad's Corvette. I took pictures and everything. Blackmail is beautiful, isn't it? She let me take her car if I promised to delete the pictures and not show Dad. I told her you and I were going to catch a movie at the Plex. I parked just down the road a little way."

"You drove here without a license?" Belmont asked, glancing at me sideways and shaking his head in clear frustration.

"Do you have a driver's license?" Jaylen retorted.

I grinned. One point for Jaylen. I shouldn't have told him all about Belmont's true age. He knew about where Belmont came from and what he did before he turned, but I kept the part about the murders of his family a secret.

"Let's just get this over with," Belmont hissed. He reached over and removed an object from the glove compartment. I couldn't immediately tell what it was, but it was small, round, and fit comfortably in his hand.

"What is that?" I asked.

Belmont paused, glanced at me, and then looked scathingly at Jaylen before opening his fingers.

It was some sort of ball with a handle. I was about to ask a follow-up question when Jaylen broke the silence.

"Is that a grenade?" he asked in astonishment.

Belmont nodded.

"Seriously?" I almost laughed, baffled. "Why did you bring a grenade?" I suddenly felt extremely alarmed. That was no toy. A grenade explosion could turn deadly real quick.

"It's a precaution," Belmont explained. "We don't know what will happen when we enter the cemetery. I want to be prepared."

"Then why not bring a gun, John Wick?" Jaylen reached for the grenade, but Belmont withdrew it. I couldn't believe how aggressive Jaylen was acting, particularly to the man who had nearly killed him not so long before. That was high school for you. We tended to easily forget things.

"I'm not familiar with how to use a gun." Belmont wrapped the grenade in a cloth and dropped it in his pocket.

"Oh, but a grenade?" I mocked. It had to be the weirdest accessory I could have ever imagined.

"And how old is that?" Jaylen asked. "What's that from? World War II?"

Belmont's face screwed up in confusion. "I'm not aware of its age."

"It probably won't work, you know?" Jaylen said. "I bet you anything, it's gone bad."

"It'll work," Belmont assured us. "And it's the best tool for the job. All I need to do is pull the pin, and the grenade will do the rest. If I come under the necromancer's spell, I may not have any time at all. Certainly not enough to point and shoot."

"Okay," I said, my voice rising with inflection. "So let's make sure if you do pull it, we're well out of range."

Belmont smiled weakly. "You have to understand something. This is my backup plan. Yes, I'm bringing this to use if I have an opportunity to stop him, but it's also to use if I've run out of options. An explosion from a grenade is not something even we can survive. So don't worry. I'll only pull the pin if I have no other choice."

Jaylen fell quiet in the back seat. I looked at him and couldn't quite tell if he had cold feet or not. I guess we all did, and not just because two of us had naturally cold feet.

The Crenshaw Mausoleum rested quietly beneath a dark, cloud-covered sky. Somewhere east of there, Gorman Randolph, the cemetery caretaker, slept next to his wife, Chloe. The old coot had no idea what abominations were taking place right under his nose. Maybe if he paid a little more attention to the maintenance around the mausoleum grounds, there wouldn't be easy access for the necromancer. Yeah, it was Gorman's fault. Sure. I could go with that.

"Jaylen, I don't remember how to open the secret entrance," I whispered.

He nodded as he led us to the eastern wall of the mausoleum and fiddled with the stone behind a patch of heavy vines. I heard a click just like I remembered from when he first showed me back in October, as he pressed the mechanism that unveiled the opening. I looked over and noticed Belmont's eyes weren't following our progression. Instead, he stood staring miserably at the entryway.

"Hey." I waved my hand until it ruptured his trance and he looked at me. "Are you going to wait right here for us until we come back?"

Belmont swallowed, his chest rising and falling rapidly. "Yes, I'll be here."

"And if you see anyone coming, what are you going to do?" Jaylen added.

Belmont's head swiveled as he looked around the perimeter of the mausoleum. "I guess if it's the caretaker, I'll hide. He's older, right?"

"Maybe seventy . . . seventy-five," Jaylen said. "He'll have a flashlight and, uh . . . oh, he sometimes walks with a cane."

I thought back to when Gorman chased me away from the mausoleum. "He'll be slow," I said. "You won't have to really run, but you'll want to draw him away from the mausoleum, so we won't get nabbed when we come out. Just don't blow him up!" I looked for the grenade, but Belmont still had it stowed away in his pocket.

He grinned awkwardly and nodded.

"Now, what if someone else comes?" This was the question we needed to ask. If the necromancer had plans to use me again as his puppet, he would more than likely enter the mausoleum through the same passage.

Belmont's face grew stern and he walked over to join us by the opening. "I won't leave you, and if he does indeed come, then we'll handle it tonight."

I took a deep breath. "What if he's down there already?"

"He's not," Belmont said.

"But how do you know?"

"You'd know it if he was close. There's no mistaking his power. It will follow him everywhere he goes, but fortunately, this will give you a warning."

"You sure you want to do this?" I turned and asked Jaylen. "Because you don't have to."

Though he looked on the verge of passing out, Jaylen

dipped his chin with a slight nod. "We're going to be famous, right? Just one question," he said. "What exactly should we be looking for when we're down there?"

Up until that moment, I hadn't really thought of how to investigate. They really didn't teach you that sort of information in school. Forensics. CSI-type junk. "I'm not sure. Maybe a footprint, or an article of clothing. Anything out of the ordinary."

Clicking on my flashlight, I gave one last look around to ensure the coast was clear, and then Jaylen and I stepped into the blackness of the mausoleum.

# Chapter 18

Everything seemed like it had been before, but the only memory I possessed of descending into the mausoleum happened in October. I didn't remember walking down these stairs as a zombie.

"This is where I should've turned back a month and a half ago. Had I done that, everything would be normal now." I whispered.

"Yeah, but hey, don't get mad at me," Jaylen said. "It was only a dare. You could have said no. It's not my fault this was your way of doing it."

"Truth or dare," I repeated, shaking my head.

I could barely see Jaylen's face peering back at me in the darkness, but I was glad he had come along.

Ahead of us, covered in moss and still wet from sprinkler water dripping down through the ground, stood an opening in the stone. It was through that opening that I first saw what I thought to be a dead body lying beneath the rubble. The collapsed rocks remained, but there was no sign of the zombie. On either side of the roof collapse, we saw two more openings. In the one on the left, I could see the outline of the Lich Stone. The flashlight's beam lit it up with an eerie glow.

Jaylen started walking toward it, but I grabbed his arm.

"No!" I snapped. "Don't go that way."

He didn't protest, but eyed the stone warily through the opening. I didn't dare chance getting close to it. Not until I could be certain we wouldn't find the necromancer hiding in the shadows.

Instead, the two of us passed by the rubble into the room on the right. Once inside, we looked at the three separate stone boxes resting across the floor. Jaylen fumbled with his flashlight, but not because of the caskets. With a shaky finger, he pointed to the corner of the room, where a familiar figure lay dormant on the ground.

The ripped shirt. The ribs jutting haphazardly out of his chest. The bone-thin arms and nearly see-through skin. No mistaking it. My friend the zombie, the one that had turned me into this abomination, lay sprawled out on the ground in front of us. The only difference, which happened to be a huge one, was the condition of the man's head.

Detached.

The zombie had been decapitated. But not in a clean way—not that there was a nice way of decapitating someone. It looked as if someone had *pulled* the head free, only it was a struggle. The top two vertebrae were torn and dislodged, jagged. Whomever, or *whatever,* had done it was frenzied.

"Holy . . ." Jaylen covered his mouth and gasped. "What is that?"

"Be quiet!" I hissed. I had to be sure. Maybe Belmont had been wrong. Maybe a zombie could still live without its head. If that were the case, we couldn't get close to it. Especially not Jaylen. I inched forward and kicked the zombie hard in the knee. The bone felt old and fragile, and the man never moved. He just lay there, lifeless. Completely dead.

After several moments in agonizing silence, Jaylen joined me at my side.

"What happened to his head?" he asked. "Did you do that?"

"No!" I said, but I wasn't entirely certain. When I had first woken up in the tomb after having encountered the zombie, the man had disappeared. Now, I understood he had only moved into the next room. Moved, but by who?

"Do you think the dude you're looking for did this? The . . . um . . .necromancer?"

"Probably," I said, my breath quivering. "Though I don't know why." We squatted there next to the ancient corpse, dragging our flashlight beams over its body like it had become some sort of wicked science project.

"Come on," Jaylen said, finishing his examination and standing up. "Let's look for clues so we can get out of here."

The room was big, and I realized it was wider than the first level of the mausoleum. It had to have been some sort of catacombs. You heard about them in ancient graveyards in Europe and places like that, but never in Jewkes.

"Check this out." Jaylen pointed to three sets of footprints on the dirty stone floor. A pair of tennis shoes, most likely mine, led out and turned toward the room on the opposite side of the wall collapse, headed for the Lich Stone. I couldn't remember passing that way, but maybe I did when I had been summoned. Behind them there was another set. Smaller, thin, with sharp, pointed toes that led me to guess they were boots—perhaps fancy ones. These had to belong to the necromancer.

The third pair of prints was a mystery. Close to mine, staggered and large, were heavy indentations in the dirt. I squatted down and shone my light on them.

Why would there be three pairs of footprints? I imagined an accomplice, someone working for the necromancer. Maybe this guy kept a lookout for the cemetery caretaker. He could've been the muscle or the protection in case things with the summoning went terribly wrong.

"Any ideas?" Jaylen asked.

I shook my head and returned my attention to the prints left by the necromancer. I stood next to them and measured the length compared to my own foot. There was really nothing I could conclude from a set of footprints. Maybe a crack team of investigators could make a plaster cast of the print or pull some sort of DNA from a strand of nearly invisible hair from the scene, but the only thing I determined from my investigation was there was a third, and we could be in serious danger.

Both of us were a little freaked out, especially with the headless zombie lying so close by, but reluctantly, we stepped up to the casket nearest the opening. I passed my fingers along the sealed edge of the lid. Gray stone, cold like the walls. How long had these things been down here? Maybe more than a hundred years. I moved the beam toward the next two caskets. They were made of the same material, but smaller, and covered in thick dirt obscuring the epitaph etched in the stone. Who were these people? Why were they hidden beneath the mausoleum?

Water dripped down from the ceiling in the corner. The drops glistened in the light, and I watched the dust scatter from the water collecting on the floor. Roots were everywhere, slinking down along the walls like long, creeping fingers. Some of the stone blocks on the wall had started to crumble. This place was old and forgotten. It was kind of sad. There were dead people lying in those caskets. Did anyone even know they were down here anymore?

"These had to belong to kids," Jaylen whispered, pointing to the much smaller caskets.

Working my hand across the surface, I removed caked dirt from the epitaph. The words were chiseled in the stone, but I could only make out some of what it said.

"Daria Wilkes, daughter of . . . someone. I can't read the next words. Can you read it?" I asked.

Jaylen cleared his throat. "God will return what was taken. Born eighteen sixty-six, died . . . eighteen-something. She was young, I think. A little girl. That sucks."

"God will return what was taken," I repeated. "What was taken?"

"A little creepy, if you ask me." Jaylen moved over to the next one. "Dacia Wilkes," he read. "Maybe they were sisters. I think they may have died around the same time."

Most of the chiseled words on Dacia's casket had been worn away. We couldn't read the catchy quote or the birth and death dates. Looking at the first casket near the entrance, the largest of the three, I could only assume it belonged to the mother. But where was the fourth? Where was the father? Maybe he had died way later in life, or maybe he had left them before they died, and that was why his casket wasn't down here with them. Maybe he . . .

An uneasy thought crept into my mind. Two daughters? A mother with no father? Hurrying over to the mother's casket, I anxiously wiped away the dust. My heart pounded. I could hear it in my temples as I read the words still legible in the stone.

"Here lies Hester Wilkes, mother of angels. Thy body shall be made whole once more." I looked up from the casket, and I was sure my eyes had grown enormous. "I know this woman."

I turned toward the door. My breath caught in my lungs, and I bobbled my flashlight, nearly dropping it.

Belmont was standing in the opening, solemnly gazing down upon the caskets.

# Chapter 19

"Belmont?" I gasped, rearing back against Hester's casket, beaming the flashlight directly in his eyes. He wasn't moving, nor had he flinched, even when I nearly cracked his skull with the flashlight. Jaylen didn't seem sure of what was going on, but he backed away from Belmont just the same.

"They're your daughters," I whispered. "Aren't they?"

Belmont's eyes blinked slowly. He didn't appear to be himself. I wondered for a moment if he even knew we were still in the room with him. Then he lifted his eyes and looked at me sadly.

"Dacia and Daria, my angels." Belmont's voice trembled, and his eyes, though incapable of crying, showed genuine pain.

"This is your family's tomb?" Jaylen asked in disbelief.

Belmont nodded. "Yes."

I pushed off from the casket and stepped reverently away. "Then this is your wife." I wasn't quite sure what to make of everything. I felt so confused, and honestly a little angry at Belmont for not telling me the truth, but I couldn't bring myself to argue with him.

"Hester." Belmont approached and placed his hands upon her casket.

I felt nauseous. It was the first time I had felt this feeling since becoming a zombie. Should've been a breakthrough for me, but I didn't care. I figured Belmont should have mentioned the significance of this place to me before I came down there.

I looked up at the ceiling and thought about the main level of the mausoleum. After all the speculation, after all the guesses by everyone in Jewkes, I knew whom the empty casket belonged to. They may not have buried Belmont in the same room as his family, but his coffin had been close.

"You lived here?" I asked. "In Jewkes?"

Belmont pressed his face against the stone and whispered something. When he finished talking, he looked at the two of us. "It wasn't Jewkes then, but yes, we lived here."

"So the necromancer that turned you into a zombie also lived here?"

Belmont's eyes shifted over to the Lich Stone.

"Why didn't you destroy it?" I asked. A brilliant idea entered my mind. I felt foolish for not thinking of it sooner. "If we break the stone, shatter it into a million pieces, won't it destroy the necromancer's power over us?" I charged out of the room toward the stone, raising my flashlight above my head in a striking motion.

"You can't!" Belmont shouted, chasing after me. Jaylen brought up the rear, though he didn't run wholeheartedly.

I swung my hand down toward it, but immediately

felt some force propel me backward. It was as though I had hit an invisible barrier protecting the Lich Stone. I tried striking again, but found myself incapable of harming it.

"We don't have the ability to destroy a Lich Stone. It's impossible," Belmont explained.

"What is that thing?" Jaylen asked. "Are those monkeys?" He leaned in close, trying to make out the images. Belmont pulled him away from it.

I slammed my flashlight against the ground in frustration, shattering the bulb. "Why didn't you tell me about this? About your family?"

"I should have told you," Belmont admitted. "But it wasn't easy."

"I get that, but I thought you couldn't come down here because you could come under the control of the Lich Stone. Was that a lie?" I still felt nauseous, but now I wanted answers.

"I'm already under its control," Belmont said, watching me closely. "It has been almost three months now since I came under the control of this Lich Stone. That is why I returned here to Jewkes."

"What do you mean?" My mind raced as I tried to piece together the mystery. "If you came under the control of the stone three months ago, then that would mean you were summoned. If he summoned you, then that would also mean he had you kill someone. The transient they found in a dumpster. I didn't kill him. You did!"

"The summoning ritual took place over several nights because I lived so far away, but the power was too strong, and I fell under the necromancer's control," Belmont said, moving toward me. "I don't know why I was told to kill him, but when I awoke in here the next morning,

I knew immediately what had happened. Someone found my Lich Stone and had figured out how to use it."

"What about the minister, Colby Martinson? I can't remember killing him. Because you're the one who did it!" It all started making sense. I should've been at a loss for words, but for some reason, they kept vomiting out of me. I pointed to the ground in front of the Lich Stone. "Those are your footprints. We've been down here together at the same time during a summoning." I laughed, even though it was far from humorous. On the contrary, I felt deceived. "You were killing people and letting me think I had committed all of the murders."

"Hold up." Jaylen raised a hand, trying to get our attention. "Did you just say all of the murders? What do you mean by that?"

I sighed, looking worriedly at him. "I guess this is my confession."

Jaylen smiled, but it faltered. "Yeah right," he said, uneasily.

"It's true." I had been dreading telling him this. There was no way we would be hanging out and watching zombie movies after that revelation.

"No, Calvin, you haven't killed anyone yet." Belmont stepped between the two of us. "That was part of my deception." He smiled grimly. "You tried to do it, and you were indeed summoned to kill the Reverend Grossier and Naomi, but somehow you broke the trance and never finished the job."

I gaped at Belmont. "But I . . . I saw her. She was dead in that fountain."

"I killed her," Belmont said. "After you failed your first assignment of killing the reverend, I was sent to finish. I woke up that night also covered in blood and still holding the reverend's head in my hands. On Sunday night, I had just cleaned up before you arrived at my place confessing to Naomi's murder. That's why I asked you if anyone else had been in the park."

"How do you know I didn't kill Naomi?" Maybe I should've dropped it and been satisfied with Belmont accepting the blame for her death, but I needed to be sure.

He reached into his pants pocket and removed a strand of pearls. The end of the necklace had been tied off to prevent the pearls from falling, but I remembered it from that night in Casper Park.

"Hester always loved pearls," Belmont said, looking toward her casket. "I hadn't killed a woman since her."

Jaylen gasped, wobbling as though on the verge of fainting. I should've gone over and steadied him, but I couldn't pull my focus away from Belmont.

"So you killed them, not me?" I asked.

Belmont chuckled softly. "I guess this proves your innocence."

I felt a flood of relief. I hadn't killed anyone. I could live with a clean conscience. All this time, I had thought I was a murderer, but it wasn't true. Under different circumstances, I might have danced around a bit, but as quickly as it appeared, the elation wore off.

"Why did you let me go around believing I had killed?" I demanded. "Were you trying to make me take the full blame?" My words echoed off the stone walls of the mausoleum.

Belmont flinched and shook his head. "That's not what I was doing. I came here to find the necromancer and to stop him. Together, we can do that now. I didn't want you to have to go through the same torture I've gone through during a summoning, and I thought maybe it would never happen. But for some reason it did, and I want to stop it. We're both in this together."

"I'm confused." Jaylen's wooziness had seemed to pass. "How did you know about Calvin?"

"What do you mean?" Belmont asked.

"His turning into a zombie. How did you know it happened?"

Jaylen's question was spot on. I had never thought to ask that before, and right now, I couldn't believe it had gone that long before surfacing. How could it be a coincidence he just happened to show up in my school? How could he know about me, about what I had become?

"I don't think now's the appropriate—" Belmont started to say, but I cut him off.

"Tell me the truth!" I demanded.

Belmont's eyes dropped. "I knew about it because I was here with you the night you first entered the mausoleum." His chest heaved. "And I was the one who killed you."

This time, Jaylen's flashlight dropped out of his hand and the bulb shattered.

# Chapter 20

I heard a ringing in my ears so loud, I couldn't help but cover them with my hands. Like a thousand tiny bells going off all at once. Belmont heard it too. It broke his concentration, and he frantically looked past me, his eyes growing with alarm. He didn't cover his ears, but dove toward me and clamped his hand over my mouth. I fought against him, wanting to pound his face, claw at his eyes, but he was too strong.

"Keep quiet!" he whispered loudly in my ear. "He's here!"

"What are you two doing?" Jaylen asked, looking from Belmont to me. He seemed oblivious to the irritating ringing sound.

"Can't you hear that?" I asked.

"Hear what?"

"That ringing!"

Belmont hushed the both of us. "No, he can't hear it, only we can."

"What is going on?" Jaylen threw his hands up in a desperate plea for information.

I was about to ask the same question, but the will to fight against Belmont vanished immediately. There was only one person who could cause that much panic in Belmont.

The necromancer had arrived. The ringing must've been the signal of his power.

"We have to get out of here now!" Belmont commanded. "We need to get above ground and hide until he enters the mausoleum, and then we need to go wake up the caretaker."

I adamantly shook my head. "That's a bad idea. Gorman will never make it here in time. I say we wait for him and take him out as soon as he pokes his face through the door." Why hide? The necromancer was coming to summon us anyway. If he succeeded in doing so, both Belmont and I would murder someone else. It was the perfect time to attack, when the creep least expected it.

Belmont seized my arm and dragged me through the doorway. I resisted and broke away from his grip. "Not here!" he said. "You can't fight him when he's near the Lich Stone. He'll be too powerful to stop."

"Use the grenade!" Jaylen whispered.

Belmont blinked and looked down to where the weapon hid in his pocket. "If we're going to stop him, we'll need to know who he is and then fight him on neutral ground. A name. A description. Maybe an address. We need to get that information first. If we stay here and try to make a stand, he'll put us under his spell as soon as he approaches the Lich Stone. If he knows we suspect him at all, he'll punish us."

"What's he going to do? Kill me?" I had been through things worse than death.

Belmont frowned grimly. "He would never do that,

but he would send you to kill your own family. And for sure, we'd be forced to kill Jaylen."

"Uh . . ." Jaylen's posture weakened. "Say that again?"

I couldn't risk hurting Jaylen, and by the looks of my best friend, he agreed wholeheartedly with the decision to exit the premises. Silently, the three of us ascended the stairs and peered out into the dark cemetery. Though the coast seemed clear, we didn't take any chances. Belmont exited first. Crouching low, he scanned the perimeter. Several tense moments passed before he motioned for us to join him. The ringing continued, but no one appeared in the clearing. Together, we raced toward the trees on the back end of the mausoleum.

Belmont was breathing heavily. "The warning sounds when he's close. He may not even be in the cemetery yet."

"How is it I don't remember the ringing from the other times I've been here?" I asked.

"You've been under the summoning power," Belmont explained. "It drowns out all other distractions."

I moved my head to the side just an inch to see past the trees. The clearing was still empty. My eyes scanned every possible hiding place. Gravestones, shrubbery, tipped-over bouquets of flowers. I didn't know what I expected to see crowning the hill, and began to imagine someone riding a black horse galloping down to the mausoleum. My ideas might have been extreme, but I was scared. Would the necromancer be tall? What would he be wearing? How would he move?

The wait was messing with my mind. I looked at Belmont for answers, but caught myself before I uttered a word. His eyes had closed, and he had his finger pressed firmly against his lips.

Someone stood in the clearing less than a hundred

yards from our tree. A cloak made of black fabric draped his body. Horrified, I watched as he moved toward the mausoleum with fast, deliberate strides. I couldn't see his feet either, but I imagined him wearing boots. The kind that left footprints with pointed toes.

There he was. Dead leaves crunched beneath his feet as he walked forward, with purpose. He was the one responsible for my grief. Perhaps he was too close to the tomb for me to attack. If what Belmont said was true, I'd be useless against him now that he was so near the Lich Stone. Still, I wanted so badly to do something. To charge after him, take him down, find a large rock and . . .

As the necromancer approached the tomb, he froze in his tracks.

Something was wrong. I could sense it, and I suspected Belmont did too. Straining my eyes, I tried to see what was causing the necromancer's hesitation. Then I saw the gaping hole emptying into the darkness of the mausoleum.

We had left the secret entryway open!

Grabbing Belmont's attention, I wordlessly mimicked pulling the pin on his grenade. He appeared to understand the gesture, but seemed unwilling to remove it from his pocket.

The necromancer's head tilted to the side as he listened. Then he turned and faced our tree. I wasn't sure if he could see us or not. We weren't moving, but if his eyes adjusted, even a little, I felt certain he'd be able to make out the outline of our figures against the backdrop of trees. The ringing had yet to stop since it first began, but like Belmont, I had managed to drown it out and keep it from distracting me. My thoughts immediately turned to my parents. I thought of how I would feel if the necromancer summoned me to torture and kill them next. I couldn't let that happen.

We were caught in a sort of silent standoff. What was the point of Belmont's weapon if he had no intention of using it?

Finally, the necromancer stepped back toward the doorway. Time was running out. I looked at Jaylen, knowing that at any moment, I would be under the Lich Stone's command. Jaylen would see me being summoned. He would see me ready to kill.

I wanted to scream at Belmont. This was our only chance.

Miraculously, the necromancer didn't enter the mausoleum. Instead, he reached out and closed the door, sealing it shut. Then, in one fluid motion, he walked away, heading rapidly toward the hill and the rear entrance.

When I felt certain we were out of earshot, I grabbed Belmont's arm. "Does he know what you drive?"

"It's doubtful," he said. "But we'll have to abandon my car. We can't take the risk."

"But can't he do some research and pull the VIN number or something?" I had heard about that on a TV show.

"*If* the vehicle were registered," Belmont said. "But it's not. Better to keep a low profile."

"What about my sister's car?" Jaylen said, then covered his mouth.

"Where did you park it?" Belmont asked, more annoyed than worried.

"Just up the road. He'll find it. He'll know who it belongs to!"

"Keep your voice down!" Belmont ordered, turning back and looking toward the mausoleum. He thought for a moment and then nodded. "Stay here and give me your

keys." He held out his hand, and Jaylen reluctantly surrendered the keys to his sister's car. "I'll pick you up out
front. Give me some time . . . maybe an hour."

He crept away, leaving the two of us behind in the
cemetery to wait for his return. It was one of the longest
hours of my life. I should have felt right at home. Jaylen
was the only one who didn't belong among the dead.

# Chapter 21

Once back in town, just outside of the Cobalt, Belmont gave Jaylen back his keys and watched as he drove away. He hadn't said much since the cemetery, but I hadn't talked his ear off either. Coming face-to-face with pure evil had a way of keeping me silent.

"It was an accident," Belmont said awkwardly as we began the long walk back to his place.

"What?" I asked, glaring at him.

"What happened to you was an accident," he said. "I never intended to kill you. When I awoke from my first summoning, I saw the man trapped beneath the rocks just like you. He begged for my help at the time, but I was too afraid and disturbed by what had happened. So I left him lying there. But then I came back. I wanted to ease his suffering. That's when I heard you coming down the secret passageway and I thought the necromancer had returned."

"So you just killed me? Just like that?" I shouted. Where was the restraint? I was a kid, for crying out loud.

"It wasn't like that. I only meant to knock you unconscious and drag you somewhere where I could question you. But when I hit you, you fell forward onto the zombie. It was he who bit you and transferred the disease.”

“Bit me?” I screwed up my face in confusion. I didn’t remember getting bit.

“Your shoulder, maybe?” Belmont asked.

I had found claw marks at the top of my right shoulder, but just thought it was from horsing around with Jaylen. “I didn’t see any bite marks, just claw marks.”

“On your back maybe,” Belmont suggested.

I turned around and lifted my shirt to show him.

“There it is.” Belmont pointed. “Bite marks.”

“And I turned just like that?” I asked. “Within seconds?”

“The changes register differently in people. It has to be blood-borne, meaning either a zombie’s saliva or blood passes directly into your bloodstream. Sometimes it can take months, even a year, for the disease to take hold. For others, not so long. But the fact that you contracted the disease in the presence of an active Lich Stone enhanced the transformation.”

“Then what?”

“I finished off that poor soul and I left you.”

I wanted to hurt Belmont for what he had done. Accident or not, he had changed my life for the worse on an impulse. But instead of tackling the old man and engaging in a fight I would most likely lose, we just walked on in silence.

“Why didn’t you throw the grenade?” I asked, after more than a mile had passed.

Belmont looked down at the road. “I need to know who he is.”

“We could’ve found that out afterward,” I said.

"When we were sifting through his body parts for his wallet."

"I need to know why he's doing this and how. Two things we would not be able to discover if he's dead. Besides, I haven't killed anyone on my own for quite some time. It's not an easy thing to do. Could you do it?"

I started to nod but thought better of it. "Probably not. But we can't worry about why he's doing this anymore. If we get a chance to ask him, great. But you have to promise to do the right thing in an emergency situation. Agreed?"

"Agreed," Belmont answered.

"How are we going to catch this creep now? You don't have a car."

"I'll get another one," Belmont interjected.

"We have no leads."

"Sure we do. We just haven't given them much thought yet. Your friend, Jaylen, is an excellent lead."

I stopped in the road, my heartbeat picking up its pace. "Jaylen's my best friend! I think I'd know if he's been dabbling in necromancy."

Belmont stroked his chin thoughtfully. "I wasn't suggesting he was the necromancer."

"Then why mention him?" I asked.

"Jaylen knew about the secret entrance into the mausoleum. How did he come by that information? No one should know about the underground tomb. It's been purposely kept secret for more than a hundred and twenty years." Belmont walked ahead, and I had to scramble to keep up.

"He overheard his dad at a poker game," I said from behind.

Belmont glanced back over his shoulder. "Who all was at this poker game?"

"I don't remember." But then I did remember someone. "Ben Nielsen, the bartender at the Cobalt, was there and he was the one who told Jaylen's dad." It was more than a revelation. I almost couldn't contain my excitement.

"I'm already aware of Ben Nielsen and his knowledge of the entryway. That's why I picked a location to eat my meals so close to the Cobalt."

"And?" I asked anxiously.

Belmont frowned. "It's not him. I doubt he has any idea what necromancer means. Who else can you remember?"

"The Randolphs, the cemetery caretakers, know about it," I said, struggling.

"Yes, they do, and no, they are not a threat."

"But how do you know?" I asked. "Mrs. Randolph has voodoo trinkets in her kitchen. I've seen them! Maybe they've been necromancers all along."

"Think about it, Calvin. When you woke up from your turning, who was the first person you met outside the mausoleum?"

"Gorman!" I said, raising my voice.

"And what did you hear?"

My forehead furrowed. "What did I hear? Nothing. He chased me away from the cemetery."

"Exactly. You didn't hear the warning chimes, did you?" Belmont asked.

My shoulders slumped. No warning chimes meant the crochety Gorman was not the necromancer. "Then we're back to square one."

Belmont shook his head curtly. "Jaylen is the link. What he knows might be the answer to who's doing this. We'll take the next few days to meet and do our research. Jaylen can come too. Especially since he's our most important lead."

I started to nod, but then shook my head instead. "I can't, remember? I'm going away with my parents on Wednesday for the holiday."

"I thought I told you that wasn't an option," Belmont said. "Being that far away from food will take its toll."

"I know, but that's why we have to meet tomorrow so I can eat. There's no time for anything else."

"You'll be vulnerable!"

"I made a choice and I'm going. And unless I'm forgetting something, you're still the jerk that caused all of this in the first place. So don't start getting bossy with me."

# Chapter 22

The flight from Lafayette Regional Airport in Louisiana to Flagstaff, Arizona, took a little over four hours. With no in-flight movie, my parents bought me a book of crossword puzzles in one of the airport gift shops.

The only mistake I made on the plane happened when I ordered a Coke from the stewardess. It was kind of my tradition. And tradition caused me to barf in the tight quarters of the airplane bathroom thirty minutes later. Soda was by far the worst thing to throw up. Pudding was pretty bad as well, but soda was violent! Fizzy, foamy, and I swear the stuff multiplied in my stomach, because I didn't remember that much Coke in my tiny plastic cup when it sat on my napkin.

My Grammy Simmons, born and raised in Louisiana, moved to Arizona two years ago for the drier climate due to her respiratory problems. I would be really excited to see her had I not been trying to unwrap the past week's events. Necromancers. Sorcery. Murders. Cannibalism. Yeah, I was aware of what most people in society considered what I did twice a week. On some remote island in the Pacific, I'd live as a headhunter, but in Louisiana . . . I didn't need to say it.

The prospect of four long days had really started to bother me while I sat in the cramped quarters of the airplane. I had done my research in case of an emergency, and there happened to be a medical training facility seven miles from my grandmother's house. They'd have cadavers. How I would get to them if the rage ever kicked in was the part I was still trying to figure out.

Belmont and I ate well the previous night: a middle-aged assembly-line worker who had died during an accident at some factory. He had been dead for almost a week and came to us a little late. Had something to do with OSHA regulations and an investigation of unsafe work conditions at the factory. But he had a nice, plump brain. Delicious. Belmont even let me have the larger portion, which included the frontal lobes. Like a finely baked casserole.

We checked into our hotel and dropped off our bags. Twenty minutes later, we arrived at the nursing home where my grandma had lived for the past six months.

*St. Bartholomew Erastus Recovery Homes.*

The place looked like an insane asylum. I'd never seen a real insane asylum in person, so I guessed it looked like an institution from a movie. White brick. Columns. Rocking chairs lined along the walls of a covered porch. I half-expected to see bars on the windows, but the white-washed shutters were just as bad. Palm trees too, sprouting everywhere along the grounds. Bushes, benches, old people pushing walkers and sprawled out on lawn furniture playing some sort of game with small, plastic tiles. I felt sorry for my grandmother. This wasn't her style, but with her breathing problems, I supposed it was for the best.

Room B35. Grammy's room. It was dark. The nurses

had drawn the shades and she was sleeping. My dad poked his head in and left Mom and me out in the hall. A couple of minutes later, he returned, looking glum.

"They've got her on some heavy sedation. She's been in a lot of pain but refuses to go to the emergency room." My dad's eyes reddened. He was going to cry. My mom hugged him and kissed his cheek, and the three of us joined him in Grammy's room.

The floor echoed as we walked, providing the only sounds in an otherwise completely silent room. They had Grammy hooked up to a monitor and an IV drip, with tubes shoved up her nostrils and under her gown. I didn't like seeing her like this. Her eyes closed. Flat on her back. We stood there for like ten minutes watching her sleep. Both my parents cried. I supposed I would've cried as well, but I couldn't physically do it.

"Mr. and Mrs. Simmons?" a doctor asked from the entry, staring at a clipboard. He looked up with an eyebrow raised.

"Yes," my mom answered.

"I'm Dr. Gomez, the head physician here at St. Bartholomew's. I've been involved in most of your mother's treatment. We're doing our best to make sure she feels comfortable." He gestured toward the door. "Perhaps we should speak outside."

That was never good. Why speak outside unless you didn't want Grammy to hear the dismal news? As my parents walked to the door, my mom looked back.

"Do you want to come with us?" she asked.

I shook my head. "I'll stay here with Grammy."

I sat down in the chair right beside her bed and tried making sense of the monitors beeping all around her. One green line kept jumping, which I supposed signaled her heartbeat.

Grammy stirred.

She made a noise like a muffled moan and her eyes fluttered. She couldn't have weighed more than ninety pounds, and she was shrinking. I could see her toes poking up at least a foot from the edge of the bed. I reached out, placing my hand on her forearm, and instantly her eyes snapped open.

Gasping, my Grammy stared down at my hand as though it were a hot iron pressed against her skin. "Get away!" she hissed, her lips curling back. "Don't you touch me!"

At first, I thought she hadn't quite woken up from her sleep, caught in some lingering nightmare. But as she yanked her arm out from under my hand, her eyes appeared fully awake and functioning.

"Grammy, it's me, Calvin." I pulled back.

She ground her teeth, and her body squirmed, writhing as if in great pain. The room seemed darker now, as though the light had been sucked out through the draped windows. I knew she shouldn't get herself this worked up, but she refused to respond to my coaxing.

"Calm down, please!"

Blood trickled out from her nostrils. I leapt up from my chair to go alert the nurses, but her fingers closed around my wrist.

"You're *rotting*," she whispered, digging her nails into my flesh. "You've come here to take something from me, but I won't let you have it. Won't give it to you. You . . ." Then she paused, and for just a moment, recognition appeared in her eyes. "Calvin?" Her gaze softened. "Where did you come from?"

My body shook. I didn't know what to expect next. I no longer felt strength in her grip, and my wrist slid free.

"Are you okay? You don't look well," she said in her familiar Southern drawl.

I tried to smile. "We just got here less than an hour ago, maybe." Was she being for real, or was this some sort of act to have me lower my guard?

Her smile widened, and she looked genuinely excited to see me. "That's right. It's Thanksgiving, and the three of you are spending it with me. We need to get out of here, out of this room and back to my kitchen. I'm going to cook you a turkey."

What had just happened? Why did she freak out? Maybe it was the meds. The doctor said she'd been under heavy sedation.

"Come closer so I can look at you. Your dad tells me you're driving now. Do you like it?"

The mood eased and the light poured in through the slats of the window blinds.

I tried controlling my breathing.

"Do you have a girlfriend?" she pressed.

I shuffled my feet. "No girlfriend." This was the Grammy I expected to meet when she opened her eyes. Interested. Eager to learn about what had been going on in my life.

"Well, get over here, Calvin," she said. I leaned forward, and Grammy propped herself up on her elbows. The tubes in her nostrils were a distraction. Blood was smeared on her top lip. Her smile glowed warm and invitingly. It reminded me of all the times we spent together over the holidays. I loved all my grandparents, but none of them quite like Grammy. There was just something about the way she looked at me as if I could do no wrong. No judgment, not like my parents. No disappointment. I could tell her anything, any of my problems, and she'd listen. I reached over to hug her, but then her eyes narrowed to thin slits, and I barely could see her pupils.

"I know what you are."

"What?" I pushed my chair back away from the bed and stood up.

"You're not my grandson. You're not my Calvin." She began to whimper. Then she started sobbing. "Not Calvin. Not Calvin. Not Calvin!" She repeated this over and over until her voice grew loud and violent.

The color drained completely from her face. She was pale and trembling, her breathing sputtering rapidly. Her eyes remained fixed on mine, watching me. When I moved, she flinched, as if terrified of what I might do.

"Grammy?" I asked.

"Devil," she exhaled sharply. "*Zonbi*!"

Her face contorted in pain as she fumbled to press the call button.

My parents and the doctor appeared in the doorway.

"John?" my grandmother asked when my dad rushed in. She looked happy to see him, and my mom as well. It was like I was not even in the room anymore, which was kind of a good thing. As long as she kept her eyes off me, maybe she wouldn't flip out.

"Mom, we're here," my dad said. They gathered around her while the doctor checked her vitals.

"All of you?" my grandmother asked.

My mom grinned and giggled. "Yes, believe it or not, Calvin has come along as well." My mom motioned for me to join them at the bedside. I didn't think it was a good idea, not with how I'd seen her react. I hesitated, but Mom insisted. "Come on. Don't make her strain her neck." I saw my grandmother's beaming face turn slowly toward me, and then the twinkle in her eyes vanished.

"Keep that *thing* away from me!" she spat through gritted teeth, and started to convulse.

# Chapter 23

I was back at the hotel. It was after midnight, and all I could think about was my psychotic grandmother. She knew what I had turned into.

*Zonbi.* That's what she had called me. How had she known? I thought about Belmont describing his last days with his wife and kids before the rage settled in and he lost control. He told me his wife could sense something had changed about him. She had been on death's doorstep, and she knew he was no longer human. I was dreading the next couple of days spending time with Grammy. How would that work? *Pass the potatoes, Zonbi! Are you enjoying Thanksgiving, you undead abomination?*

My parents had been asleep for almost an hour. They had thought Grammy had acted strange, but the doctor blamed it on hallucinations brought on by the strong sedative. Hallucinations, my eye. That woman was completely sober. She saw through everything.

My stomach felt empty. I had just eaten last night, but already I craved a bite. I wouldn't get another meal until Sunday evening. That was too far away and too long to wait. My head grew heavy. I felt dizzy and disoriented. Was it exhaustion? How was that even possible? Zombies didn't feel exhaustion.

My eyes closed, and I was no longer in the hotel.

Dripping water. Fog. Whispering. I could see the Lich Stone standing in the center of the tomb, along with the caskets of Belmont's dead family members. And there was the necromancer. He was facing the stone, and I stood behind him. I had never been in that position before. From this new vantage point, I realized the necromancer's cloak wasn't actually black. It was a dark burgundy, and I could see rips in the fabric and strands of cloth where it had frayed at the bottom. He looked dirty. He was covered in cobwebs. His hands were stretched out in front of him, and I could see his thin fingers.

The whispering grew louder, stronger. I felt drawn to his voice, but somehow, I was able to keep myself from walking forward.

Then Belmont entered the room and moved beside me. He walked past, showing no recognition. His eyes were white orbs in dead sockets, no pupils. I tried calling out to him, to stop him from obeying the necromancer's commands, but I couldn't speak.

The words grew stronger in my ears until the stranger no longer whispered.

Then my eyes opened, and I found myself back in the hotel. I could hear my parents' soft breathing in the bed next to me. I looked down at my clothes, expecting to see carnage, but I found myself clean. No blood. No tattered fabric from an innocent victim.

I scanned the room and saw the television, the dresser, our suitcases. I was definitely back, but how could I be? How could I have moved so fast to be in the mausoleum and then back in the hotel? It wasn't possible, but

I couldn't dwell on that fact. At that moment, I realized someone else was standing in our hotel room. The necromancer stood hunched by the window, his cloaked head barely beneath the lamp. Just like before, in the mausoleum, he had his arms outstretched and he was whispering. I could see his eyes glowing red beneath the shadow of his hood.

My throat constricted and my hands balled up into fists. How did he get here? He must have followed me, but I knew that couldn't be right. Without the power of the Lich Stone, he couldn't command me here. Unless . . . unless he discovered some other way. That would mean his powers had grown stronger and that Belmont and I were no longer safe wherever we went.

Yet something felt different. The necromancer's voice didn't appear to carry from his lips. I sat up and leaned forward, terrified, noticing the haze lingering around his body. Standing, I looked down at my parents to make sure they were still alive—they were, thank goodness—then moved toward the necromancer.

There was this strange sensation, a tugging in my stomach behind my belly button, like the connection to an umbilical cord. As I moved closer, the tugging weakened, and as my eyes focused, the necromancer vanished. Not in a poof of smoke like some cheap magician's trick. He was just no longer there. In fact, I knew he had never been there. My mind had conjured the image. Perhaps he had been trying to summon me again, but my hotel was too far away.

I should've felt relieved, but I didn't. Instead, my hunger almost overtook me. For a fleeting moment, I stared at my parents sleeping peacefully and wondered what their brains would taste like.

"Stop it!" I hissed to myself. I had to keep calm and

in control. I could fight the urge. Sitting on my bed, I occupied my time with a crossword puzzle and tried to remember the taste of cheeseburgers.

# Chapter 24

Saturday.

Just one more day of this hell, and then I'd be headed home. This trip couldn't end quickly enough. Thanksgiving had come and gone. No incidents with Grammy because she hadn't been there. Later that night, after we had visited her, she slipped into a coma. No one believed me when I told them I caused it, but I did. My aura had made her wig out and go crazy. I gave her a nosebleed, probably caused her brain to hemorrhage. Yeah, she was dying before we got there, but I just sped up the process.

The one silver lining—if you could call it that—was that after we got to the hotel, I insisted on calling her. The call was brief, but she wasn't able to detect what I was through the phone. My grammy was as sweet as ever, but her voice was strained. She took shallow breaths every few words. At least I was able to tell her I loved her and she said it back. But the outcome was the same—she was comatose an hour later.

On Thursday night, for our big holiday dinner, my parents and I ate at a buffet. Buffets were the creations of cruel, heartless people. So much food, and I couldn't taste any of it. They spent most of the next two days at the hospital with Grammy, while I hung out at the hotel watching television, doing crossword puzzles, and blocking all thoughts of murdering my parents for their brains from my head. I was sad to say it wasn't easy.

While sitting alone, surfing through the hotel's extensive array of television channels—they offered sixteen, and three of those were Spanish stations—the phone rang. It wasn't the hotel phone, but my mother's cell. She had left it with me in case I needed to get ahold of her for an emergency.

I didn't recognize the number, but picked it up anyway.

"Hullo?" I asked.

"Uh . . . hu . . . hullo? I might have the wrong number. I'm trying to get ahold of Janice Simmons," a voice answered on the other end.

"This is her phone," I said. "You called the right number."

"Calvin?"

"Yep." Still didn't know who it was, but I was growing warm with my guesses.

"It's Miriam Monroe. How are you . . . how are you guys doing?"

Mrs. Monroe? It was Jaylen's mom. She hardly ever called my mother, which made this more than a little odd.

I sat up on the bed and muted the television. "I'm doing okay."

"Good. That's good. Can I speak to your mother?"

"She's not here," I said.

"Oh dear. Well is there a way to reach her?" Mrs. Monroe asked. "This is kind of an emergency." She sounded distressed, and she spoke rapidly.

"She's at the hospital with my dad. What's happened?" I wondered if something had happened to Jaylen.

Mrs. Monroe sighed, whispered to someone on the other end, probably her husband, and then said, "I guess you'd find out from someone anyway. I just hate to be the one who tells you."

"What is it?" I demanded. She needed to get on with it already!

"Someone broke into your home last night. They shattered one of the little side windows by the door and undid the deadbolt. You guys really need a security system. It's not safe not having one."

I bolted upright completely. "We were robbed?" I exclaimed.

"Oh see, honey, I shouldn't be the one telling you this. I don't know what they took or if they took anything at all. I'm guessing it would be foolish of them to break in if they weren't going to make off with some of your valuables, but like I said, I'm not the right person to give you the details. I just wanted to make sure your mother knew. Your neighbors called the police, and they're investigating it right now. Does your father have his cell phone on him?"

This was unbelievable. Robbed? We had never been robbed.

"Calvin?" Mrs. Monroe's voice grew louder. "You still there?"

"Yes," I replied, annoyed. Who would want to steal from us? We didn't own anything worth taking. I mean, I had some possessions in my room that would send me into a zombie rage if someone had stolen them.

"Do you have his number?" she pressed. "Maybe I should call him and tell your folks what happened."

I gave her the number and then asked if Jaylen was

home. As soon as I hung up with Mrs. Monroe, I called their home number and Jaylen answered.

"I figured you'd be calling," he said as soon as he picked up.

"We were robbed?" I asked.

"I guess."

"What did they take?" I performed a silent inventory in my mind.

"How should I know? I don't know what you own. Besides, no one's been allowed to get close to the house while the police are searching for evidence."

I started to laugh. I couldn't think of anything else to do. It was hilarious. No one in our neighborhood had ever been robbed.

Jaylen laughed as well. We were a couple of dips, laughing about a robbery. "The question now is, do you have any enemies in the circus?" he asked.

I snorted and laughed even louder. "What does that mean?"

"The circus," he repeated.

"I heard you the first time, but why the circus?"

"You've got a freak staking out your house. I talked to your neighbor, Mr. Fleming, and he told me he saw the whole thing. Saw some guy wearing a black robe with a hood break the window and then let himself in. Dude belongs in a circus." He continued to laugh, but I no longer felt in the mood.

"Black robe with a hood?"

"Yeah."

"Jaylen." It was the only word I needed to say, and he finally caught on.

"Oh balls! I never thought about that!" Jaylen blurted out. "Is it him? The necromancer?"

"Who else would be wearing a cloak?"

Jaylen groaned through the receiver. "Why would he be at your house? How does he know where you live? Does this mean he knows where I live?" He seemed destined to ask a million questions, but I stopped him.

"Calm down!"

"Calm down?" Jaylen's voice grew louder.

"Yeah, I'm the one who got robbed, remember? This could be a good thing."

"How is this a good thing?"

"Maybe the police will catch him," I said.

Jaylen exhaled a sigh of relief. "Of course they'll catch him. I'm sure the moron left fingerprints all over your house. Besides, Sheriff Carlson is personally overseeing the whole investigation."

"Sheriff Carlson? Why should that make me fell all warm and fuzzy?" I knew who Sheriff Carlson was, but his name didn't immediately flash an image of a crack detective in my head. Plus, just Jaylen mentioning him conjured up another memory that teased at the edge of my mind.

"He's like my dad's best friend, or was his best friend in college. That guy's a stud."

That did make me feel good, but still, the name Sheriff Carlson lingered awkwardly. "Okay, cool. Do me a favor. You have to find out whatever you can about the investigation."

"I'm on it, bro."

"I'll be home tomorrow night, and then we'll need to hook up and go over everything." How did the necromancer know where I lived? Was running background checks on minion zombies standard procedure nowadays? Was this the type of behavior I could expect to happen again when my family and I were home? He must've been looking for me and wondering why I never showed when he summoned me the other night. Things had just entered a whole new level of weird.

"You know what?" Jaylen asked. "Ah, this is perfect. I'll find out a bunch of stuff tonight when the sheriff gets here."

"Gets where?" I asked.

"My house."

"Why would he be coming to your house?"

Jaylen chuckled. "It's Saturday, man! Poker night. Sheriff Carlson never misses a chance to take my dad's money."

When I hung up the phone, I sat on the hotel bed and felt a strange pit form in my stomach. The necromancer knew where I lived. He would be back, that much was for certain. I needed to talk to Belmont, and the wait was going to drive me insane.

# Chapter 25

When we arrived back at our house late Sunday evening, good ole Sheriff Harold Carlson stood waiting for us in our driveway.

"Always fun to come home from vacation to something like this, isn't it?" he asked. He winked at me and shone his flashlight on the cracked window by the front door, illuminating the entry point the necromancer had used to enter the house.

Sheriff Carlson was a tall, thin man with broad shoulders and scruff on his chin. He had gray hair, tired blue eyes, and a moustache that he kept neatly trimmed.

The sheriff led us into the house to make sure we felt safe, and my mother clicked on the living room light.

"Do we know if he took anything?" she asked.

*Chimes!* I stared at the officer. The chimes were back—distant, but back. My heart would have raced if I could feel it. I stared at him, studying his face. It had to be him. The necromancer.

"I'm afraid there wasn't enough clear-cut evidence to determine that." Carlson clicked off the flashlight.

"Doesn't look like it, though. There are no signs of a robbery, other than the cracked window, which could be explained by a number of things. Paperboy chucked too hard, some kid's baseball, suicidal birds . . ."

The moment he spoke, the chimes stopped. That was odd . . .

"Birds?" I said, suspiciously.

Carlson's eyes brightened. "I'm just saying, for all we know there wasn't even a break-in."

The warning chimes started, then stopped again the moment the officer spoke. I held my head, trying to understand, but my stomach growled, and I couldn't stay focused.

"But Mr. Fleming said he saw . . ." my dad started to say, and the sheriff held up his hand to stop him.

"I know what he said he saw, and we're investigating this as such. The way I figure, there probably was somebody snooping around. Fleming said he saw someone in the yard looking through the windows, but all the bedroom doors are closed and your front door was still deadbolted from the inside. We only opened it because you gave us permission to enter the other night. Probably some kid planned to rob you, even went as far as breaking the glass, but I'm guessing he chickened out."

"Do we have a description of the burglar?" my mom asked.

Sheriff shook his head. "It was dark, of course, and Fleming swears the guy was wearing some sort of Halloween costume. But then again, it could've been one of the get-ups kids wear these days. I dunno. Some sort of long coat, maybe a robe. Hooded."

"Really?" my mom asked, gripping the handrail of the stairs. Hooded burglars didn't exactly evoke warm, fuzzy feelings. "You don't think it could've been the same one who's been doing all those killings in Jefferson, do you?"

The continuous start and stop of warning chimes pushed my anxiety to a ten. Someone had broken in, and this bozo didn't seem to care. Worse, this bozo could be the necromancer.

Upon hearing this, the sheriff chuckled. "No, ma'am, I do not. I reckon those are unrelated. But don't worry. I really don't think he ever came in. We dusted the place for prints." He sighed, bored. "It's clean."

"And you've checked the *whole* place for prints?" I asked in disbelief. My parents both looked at me, a little astonished by my tone. But it just seemed odd that they checked the whole place for prints. Of course there would be prints. Wouldn't there? Ours would still be there, as well as any of my parents' friends who happened to stop by in the past week or two.

"Uh-huh." The sheriff folded his arms.

"The whole place?" I clarified, staring closely at the handrail leading up the stairs. A thin layer of dust appeared easily visible to all, but I doubted it came from any investigation.

"I don't think I understand what you're getting at," he said.

"Maybe I don't either," I said abruptly.

"Calvin, what's gotten into you?" my mom asked.

What's gotten into me? The truth? The officer might or might not be the one summoning me to become a murderous zombie and was casing me and our house in broad daylight. Oh, and I was starving. I hadn't eaten in four days. The beginnings of the rage could be kicking in, and then no one would be safe from my wrath.

Plus, this little robbery put a damper on my Sunday-night meal. There was no way my parents would be going to sleep anytime soon, so Belmont would have to eat without me. And right now, I firmly believed Sheriff Carlson was full of it, possibly in on it. They hadn't performed a proper investigation. The necromancer walked right into our house, probably went to my room—lay on my bed—and that idiot had no way of knowing it. I didn't say any of this, of course, because I still had a tiny bit of respect for authority. A teeny, tiny bit.

Sheriff Carlson smiled. "Don't worry about it, ma'am. Calvin, is it?" He nodded at me. "You're right. We didn't dust the whole house. Just around the door and around any area a typical burglar would contact upon entering your home. It all came up clean as a whistle. Chances are your neighbor made a mistake and only thought he saw someone come into your home."

"Or this burglar's really good at covering his tracks," I suggested.

Silence. The chimes stopped. I eyed the sheriff. I needed to talk to Belmont.

"That's enough, son," my dad said, obvious annoyance in his voice.

An arrogant twinkle formed in the sheriff's eye. "I reckon he's a little uptight that some of his belongings might be missing. I guess I'd be the same. Well, Calvin, go on." He nodded toward the stairs. "Search your room. Make sure all your video games are in their proper place. Be sure to go through all of your drawers and count your socks."

I wanted to argue further but I didn't. Instead, I climbed the stairs and left my parents to deal with the obnoxious Sheriff Carlson.

Later that night, my parents and I stayed up to do a full inventory of our belongings. All of our electronics, my mother's jewelry, and my dad's tools were still in the

house. I knew that would be the case, because the necromancer was not some common thief. He had a motive,
but I had no idea what. And though my stomach rumbled
all night as I lay in bed and daydreamed of soft, squishy,
delectable brains, I managed to keep my murdering urges
under control.

# Chapter 26

I ditched school after lunch to meet Belmont at his place, and to my relief, he had saved the body from the previous night. The brain still tasted fresh, and it wasn't even leftovers.

We ate hastily. Poor Mr. Burgess. He died from complications of pneumonia and probably never expected this to happen to his head. Then we headed to the public library. While my food settled, I thought about what had happened the day before with Sheriff Carlson. Had I really heard chimes, or was it just the hunger taking over? I decided to hold off on saying anything until we did our research. I knew the chimes didn't go in and out, and I couldn't be positive it even happened.

Over the weekend, Belmont had purchased a newer used car from a shady lot—a nice silver Buick with tinted windows. The man had loads of money, and he purchased that one right off the lot with cash, giving a little extra to keep it "between them." Where did Belmont find these people?

We ducked down at a table near the periodical section

and made a list of all the names of the recently murdered. Naomi Dansbury was the last to die. Belmont thought there would have been more, but something went awry during the summoning Wednesday night when I was in Arizona. My little vacation saved us from another murder. My absence messed things up for the necromancer, and I felt overjoyed.

I couldn't say the list made sense, but Naomi was definitely a piece that didn't add up. Why her? Colby Martinson and S. Maxwell Grossier were religious men. Had she been religious too? Of course, trying to find a pattern proved pointless, because the transient, George Oldman, also poked holes through everything. He wasn't even originally from Jewkes or Jefferson. In fact, according to his most recent records, George was a regular attendee at a soup kitchen in Atlanta, Georgia.

"I just don't get it," I said, dropping a newspaper on the table and rubbing my eyes in frustration. "This guy doesn't make any sense. And did you read that thing about his finger? That's kind of weird." I was referring to a little side article I read on how the transient had been apparently mugged by a stranger right before his murder, and the mugger cut off George's finger. Not something you read about every day.

Belmont glanced at the article and wiped his mouth. "Yeah, I read it, and I've been thinking about him a lot lately. I think he does make sense."

"How?"

"I think our necromancer is not some all-powerful sorcerer. I think he stumbled upon the craft, maybe even by mistake," Belmont explained. "Naturally, he wouldn't want to try out this new power without first attempting it on someone insignificant. Somebody no one would miss."

"Homeless people aren't insignificant," I said. "That guy probably had a family at one time!"

Belmont rolled his eyes. He could do this much better than me, which made me jealous. "Save the human-rights argument for some other day. I'm just stating the facts as the necromancer would see them."

"So our transient was a trial run," I agreed. "Test subject. Then we've got two churchy fellas and some woman in a park."

Belmont fell silent once more as we both read, rifling through newspapers and looking at public-access records. I held up the front page of the *Jefferson Gazette* dated Wednesday, November 26. The headline read, "Hundreds Attend Funeral of Slain Local Sweetheart." I'd already read this article back at my house, and from what I could see, it contained nothing of value other than a picture of Naomi's graveside service. I felt a lump form in my throat as I thought of all the people mourning her senseless death. Several people in the picture were dressed in black and standing solemnly while the casket was lowered at the cemetery. One of the many grieving was a weeping Garrett Dansbury, Naomi's husband. My heart went out to him. There were two women standing to his left with veiled faces. Everyone looked so exhausted and sad. I almost tossed the depressing picture aside, but then I noticed someone standing behind Garrett, wearing sunglasses, sporting a moustache and still in uniform. It was none other than Sheriff Carlson.

Why would the sheriff attend Naomi's funeral?

"Did you see this?" I asked, flashing the picture for Belmont to see.

He nodded. "Yes, I read it. Why?"

I pointed to the image of Sheriff Carlson, and Belmont's eyes narrowed with suspicion. He reached for the paper and leaned in for a closer look.

"That's not his jurisdiction, is it?" I asked.

"No, it isn't."

"I knew it!" I snapped my fingers, shouting a little too loudly and causing a concerned look from the librarian.

"Quiet!" Belmont hissed.

"This all makes sense now. I wasn't hearing things!" I almost couldn't contain my excitement as I realized something critical to our investigation. Jaylen had already given it to me, but at the time, it had failed to register. "Sheriff Carlson knows about the secret passage beneath the Crenshaw Mausoleum."

"How do you know that?" Belmont asked anxiously.

"Jaylen told me the sheriff is one of the regulars at his dad's poker game. I can't believe I forgot about that. And yesterday, when he was at our house, I heard the warning chimes."

"What?" Belmont frowned. "Why didn't you tell me that?"

"I wasn't sure. It was different. I thought maybe I was hallucinating from the hunger. But they were there, on and off."

"On and off?" Belmont raised an eyebrow. "That's not how it works, Calvin."

"But it did. I swear to you," I said. "It was kinda faint at first, then it grew louder. When the sheriff spoke, it stopped. Like someone hit mute. Then . . . BAM! When he stopped, the chimes were back."

"That's a strong lead. I can't deny it," Belmont said. "It *could* be him. Or the necromancer was close, hiding somewhere."

"What do we do?" I asked.

"Before we do anything rash, we need to be sure."

"I'm telling you, it's him. It all adds up." I leaned back in my chair and crossed my arms.

Belmont nodded.

We spent the next hour researching, and discovered Harold Carlson was actually Naomi's uncle on her mother's side.

"All right, then, what does this mean? Is he our guy?" Anxiety rose in my throat. If it was him, then we shouldn't waste any more time.

"Maybe. The evidence isn't in his favor." Belmont glanced at the article for another minute and then folded it, sliding it out of the way.

My mind recalled the incident with the sheriff in my home the previous night. How things didn't match up and how everything seemed so suspicious. "I think he could be," I said. "He's cocky enough to think he could control a zombie."

"If he is, then this becomes trickier than before," Belmont said. "He's a man of the law and someone skilled in investigating crime scenes. Which means he probably knows how to cover his tracks."

I snapped my fingers again and almost blurted out my words for a second time, but managed to control my excitement. "But that makes so much sense! That's why they didn't find any traces of a break-in at my house. Even if he did leave prints, he was the one dusting the place. It's the perfect cover-up." This felt like a major victory.

"It still doesn't make this any easier."

"Really? Five minutes ago, we had no clue of who to suspect. Now we have a serious lead. A master at sneaking in would have no trouble moving in and out of the cemetery or someone's house. The chimes. It's all adding up. All we have to do is catch him."

"Think about it, Calvin. In order to stop the necromancer, we're going to have to kill him." Belmont leaned forward to whisper. We looked around to make sure no one passing by happened to be listening in. "But how can we prove he's the guilty one? If we kill him, we could get caught, and if we don't have any proof, then we'll be blamed for all the murders."

"What evidence is there?"

Belmont looked up at the ceiling, pondering. "There will be evidence," he said softly. "A necromancer has to use something of the victim as a trigger. Something his servants can home in on and track."

"Like clothing, or skin, or hair?" I just figured out an odd correlation between zombies and bloodhounds. Irrelevant and pointless to dwell on considering the mess I was currently in, but it was also kind of interesting too. I possessed this innate ability to sniff an object and locate its owner. There had to be some way I could use that to my advantage once this whole necromancer business blew over.

"Not clothing," Belmont said. "Only something from the victim's actual body can be used as a trigger, and it has to be something substantial. A simple strand of hair will not work. For example, if he uses blood as his trigger, then it would have to be a lot of blood—maybe a pint the victim gave as a donor. Or if the trigger *is* hair, he could've found enough at a barbershop or a salon to use."

I swallowed. A pint of blood? The necromancer had given me a pint of blood on the night I was summoned to kill the reverend. Though I hadn't gone through with it, I had come close. Then I remembered the hair I had found closed within my fingers the night of Naomi's murder. She had short hair when I attacked her, and that would explain why the lock of hair had been long. The necromancer had probably taken it from a beauty salon or wherever she went to have her hair done. This guy could go anywhere, and with the use of his zombies, could kill anyone. So far, I had managed to keep from slaying innocent people, but I feared my luck would soon run out.

Belmont folded up the newspaper and stacked the books neatly on the table. "It's likely the sheriff has kept these triggers."

"What for? Mementos?" What kind of sick, sick, sicko was this guy?

"He needs to keep them to help maintain control over his zombies and the Lich Stone. He will have learned this from his reading. It's part of the sorcery. But if we can find those and somehow reveal the evidence to the right authorities, we could lead them to him."

"Then we wouldn't necessarily have to kill him!" I almost said this too loudly again.

Belmont's eyes dropped. "Oh, we'll have to kill him. Make no mistake. As long as he's breathing, he's a danger to our kind. He's tasted the power of necromancy and will crave it uncontrollably. If we don't kill him, he'll find a way to tap back into the source of that power."

I sighed. "When do we do this?"

Belmont checked his watch and glanced toward the door.

I followed his eyes. "What? Now?"

He nodded.

"Shouldn't we wait until tomorrow? You know, think this thing through after a good night's rest?"

"We don't sleep," Belmont reminded me.

"You know what I mean."

"The necromancer broke into your house the other night."

"Yeah, I know, he's getting desperate," I said.

"It's not just that. He was in your house. Why do you think that is?"

"I guess I probably ticked him off when I didn't show up the other night to the summoning." Where was Belmont going with this?

"Or maybe he was looking for something to use on you."

"Use on me?" I flinched. "I don't follow."

"Something of your parents' maybe. Something personal to use as a trigger."

"You mean to . . ." But I didn't need to finish the sentence. If the necromancer had taken something from my family, then there was only one thing he intended to do. Tonight might be the night I killed my parents.

# Chapter 27

Belmont's car idled next to the entrance of a cul-de-sac two doors down from Sheriff Carlson's house. School hadn't even let out yet, and no one appeared to be home at the Carlsons'. It looked like a nice place. Big yard. Wraparound porch. They owned a brick mailbox and one of those little gnome statues out on the lawn. Not what I would have typically had in mind when picturing the lair of a powerful devil wizard, but I was wearing a Run-D.M.C. T-shirt and light gray Chuck Taylors. And I was a zombie. Lesson? I shouldn't judge a book by its cover.

The sheriff was married to a florist, and we guessed she wouldn't be home until later. It was only a guess, though. Plus, his kids had all moved away. We did our research before driving out here. We weren't that stupid.

As I watched the house, checking for signs of movement just in case he had a houseguest lazing around, I also scanned for any proof of a security system or any of those stickers people liked to place in the windows to ward off trouble. I couldn't see any. I mean, he was the sheriff. What did he have to worry about?

Five minutes passed. My heart wasn't acting normal. I had never heard it pound so loudly before. It was like an angry animal stuck in a cage. My hands started to shake as well—not as badly as they did when Grammy wigged out, but close enough. I couldn't believe what we were about to do. Up to this point in my life, I had a clean record. I had never even shoplifted before. That might sound like a strange thing to say, but as I contemplated breaking into the sheriff's home with every intention of killing him, my mind was dwelling on odd things.

"Why can't we do this at night?" I asked. "There's nowhere to hide out in the open."

"First of all, he'll be home at night. Which won't give us much time to find evidence. And secondly, you don't want to do this at night. A necromancer's power is greater once the sun goes down. I'm not saying Carlson is all-powerful. Chances are, he's only mastered the use of the Lich Stone, but we can never be too sure."

"Maybe that explains why the chimes weren't constant," I said. "It was the middle of the day."

"Possibly," Belmont said flatly.

Drumming my fingers on the dashboard, I went back to watching the house. What if the neighbors saw us? Would they call the . . . I guess they'd call Carlson. I found that hilarious, but I only enjoyed the thought briefly as Belmont shut off the car and got out.

We moved stealthily across the road and down the driveway along the side of the house. The curtains had been pulled open, and I could see straight into the living room. I chanced pressing my face against the glass for a better look. The home looked even nicer on the inside. Carlson owned a massive bookshelf with all manner of hardbound books. A television rested in front of a sectional couch and a grandfather clock stood in one corner, ticking away the seconds until my destruction.

I pulled back from the window intent on asking Belmont a question, but he was already gone.

"What the—" I started to whisper, but stopped when something caught my attention out of the corner of my eye. I looked back through the window and saw Belmont waving at me from inside the living room.

"You don't waste any time, do you?" I asked after joining him through the unlocked back door. People in Jewkes were just too trusting. You should always keep all doors locked, just in case a couple of intelligent zombies were in the neighborhood. Maybe intelligent was being too generous. At least one of us was intelligent. The other one was named Belmont.

Belmont was all business now. Together, we headed straight upstairs to the bedrooms. There were three of them, along with two bathrooms and an office. Belmont assigned me the task of checking the master bedroom while he rummaged through the desk in the office. Neither one of us had any idea what we were looking for.

As I had hoped, the master bedroom was empty. Sheriff Carlson owned a king bed, a dresser, and an armoire that opened, revealing a hidden television set. Blankets and extra pillows filled a large footlocker at one end of the bed. Two nightstands rested on either side, one with a lamp and an alarm clock. I found nothing worth noting, and more of the same in the walk-in closet. As I started sifting through Carlson's shirts, I realized unless he was hiding a human scalp under the lapels of his sport coat, there was really no point in searching in here. I examined a couple pairs of boots. Sniffed them. I didn't know why, because I couldn't smell, but I was trying to enter full bloodhound mode.

I discovered a small steel safe hidden next to a stack of picture albums. After fiddling with the combination for a while, even going as far as pressing my ear against the door like they did in movies to listen for a click, I had no luck in opening it.

I felt my impatience growing. I was agitated, annoyed, disgruntled even. We were in the sheriff's house illegally, and Belmont had me wasting my time searching through the man's wardrobe.

"Anything?" Belmont asked from behind. I jerked around and clutched at my chest.

"Hey, how about a signal before you come in here and scare the crap out of me?" I shouted. "There's nothing in here."

He looked down at my lap and made a face. I was holding one of the albums, opened to Carlson's wedding pictures. "This isn't weird," I said, trying to sound as convincing as possible. "I'm looking for clues. What did you find in the office?"

Belmont squatted and thumbed through one of the other albums. "I think he must have another location. It wouldn't make sense for him to keep any of his materials out in the open where his family could happen upon them."

"Yeah, I bet he's stashed them outside in a shed or something. Should we go check . . ."

The garage door rumbled open downstairs as a car pulled in.

Belmont's eyes widened, and I looked at him in desperation. Someone was home. Was it the sheriff?

We moved to the bedroom door and cautiously peered around the corner.

Footsteps in the kitchen. Light ones, not heavy. A woman's, maybe?

She tossed her keys on the kitchen table, humming to herself. Then she said something, her voice soft and cheery, and we both froze. Had both of the Carlsons come home early for the day? That would throw the world's biggest wrench into our plans. When she continued to speak, but no one replied, I realized she must be talking to a pet. Maybe her cat. I remembered seeing a food bowl on the kitchen floor when we first entered the house.

"What do we do now?" I whispered.

Belmont fixed me with a stern look to keep quiet.

Mrs. Carlson started rummaging in the refrigerator. She placed a glass on the table, filled it with something, drank, and then walked casually toward the living room. From where we stood, we could see her by the stairs. If she looked up, we'd be spotted for sure, but she was too preoccupied with reading her mail to notice. A petite woman, Mrs. Carlson had short blond hair, though it had gray throughout, fashioned into a bun.

Belmont and I stepped back into the room. We had to get out of here, but that woman blocked our exit. If she caught us in the act, our whole plan was ruined.

I followed Belmont to the other side of the bedroom. Quietly, he tugged open the blinds and examined the window. It opened to the side, and there was a screen we'd have to mess with, but worse was the long drop down to the ground below. Maybe twenty feet. At that height, we'd break our legs for sure and be forced to hobble away in plain sight of everyone in the neighborhood.

Whose bright idea was it to sneak into Carlson's house anyway? I was pretty sure it wasn't mine. I hoped

Belmont had some sort of a plan, but he looked desperate and confused.

Then there were footsteps on the stairs.

We had no time to escape out the window. We had to hide! Belmont pointed to the closet and I didn't hesitate. Tiptoeing as quietly as possible across the bedroom, I pulled the closet door shut just as Belmont slid under the bed and Mrs. Carlson, obviously hard of hearing, entered the room.

The closet was pitch black, and I had to be careful I didn't tip over the stacks of picture albums or a pair of Carlson's shoes. Plus, where was I going to find any cover in here? In fact, I really wouldn't have called it a walk-in closet. I felt my grasp on my wits weakening, but I calmed myself, trying to listen and pinpoint Mrs. Carlson's precise location in the room.

I heard running water in the bathroom sink. Maybe she would take a shower? But the water shut off and then I heard her footsteps leave the bathroom. The armoire opened. Closed. She sat on the bed and I heard the groaning of mattress and box springs. She kicked her shoes off on the floor and plopped down on the pillows.

A nap? Was she taking a nap? That might work. How would I know if she fell asleep? I'd have to let her lie there for a good fifteen minutes before I chanced opening the closet, and then be ready to dash if she wasn't completely under. But I could do it. I was willing to wait.

And then suddenly, I became fully aware of a small shadow dancing around near the crack at the bottom of the door. I focused in on it and noticed furry paws digging at the carpet close to where I stood, and then I heard the bell of a pet collar jingling. It was the stupid cat!

"Did you find something?" Mrs. Carlson whispered. The mattress groaned again, and a much larger shadow joined the cat outside the closet door. I held my breath as the cat continued to paw at the opening.

"What is it?" she asked. Her voice prodded the cat to scratch more violently. "Is it a mouse?" I took a step back and kicked over the photo albums. The pawing stopped and the cat hissed as my breath released in a loud, harsh burst.

"Hello?" the woman called out, her tone slow and deliberate. She didn't sound worried yet, just curious. I wondered if she expected to find her husband playing a trick on her behind the door. She would probably toss that dumb cat right in my face when she saw me. I considered charging out before she got a chance to open the closet. Maybe I could knock her over and somehow make it down the stairs and out the door before she recovered from the shock and identified me as I escaped.

The doorknob swiveled and the closet opened just a crack. I couldn't do it. I couldn't run! My feet felt cemented to the floor. As the door pushed forward wider, I was given less than a second to snatch one of Sheriff Carlson's sports jackets off the closet rack and cover my face.

Mrs. Carlson laughed. She looked right at me and laughed. Definitely not the reaction I expected. Still, I clung to the jacket, keeping my face covered. Her laugh grew stronger for a second as she took a step forward, but then it tapered off completely.

"Uh . . . excuse me?" she asked, her voice now anxious, wavering. She gasped. The cat's hissing sounded like the gas leaking from a busted pipe. "What is this . . ." Mrs. Carlson began to back away. "What are you doing in my house? Who are y . . ." I heard her words suddenly dissolve into a garbled sound of choking. I expected to hear a scream for help. To hear her charging toward the phone and call her husband, but she didn't. She was gasping. Struggling. The cat shrieked and bolted from the room. Confused, I lowered the jacket and my mouth gaped open.

Belmont was straddled on top of Mrs. Carlson, choking her from behind. His weight had overpowered her. Her eyes had closed and her mouth, like a fish, frantically sucked for air. She dug her fingernails into Belmont's forearm, clawing, raking away deep grooves of skin, but he held tight until her body fell limp and the struggle ceased.

"Are you out of your mind?" I finally found the ability to scream. "You killed her!"

Belmont panted and I shoved him away from Mrs. Carlson's limp body. Listening to her chest, I wondered if I would be able to resuscitate her. I settled down once I heard the slow toll of her heartbeat. She wasn't dead, just unconscious.

"We've got to move!" Belmont ordered.

Mrs. Carlson's head shifted. She groaned as she started to come to.

With Belmont in the lead and me nipping at his heels, we ran as fast as we could. I had no idea if Mrs. Carlson had gotten to her feet yet, but I wasn't about to wait and find out. We hit the pavement at an all-out sprint. One of Mrs. Carlson's neighbors was busy out in the yard, kneeling down in one of the flowerbeds. She turned to look as we breezed past.

Belmont turned the key in the ignition, and as the tires squealed, propelling us down the street, I watched over the back of the seat as Mrs. Carlson stumbled out onto the wraparound porch, barking loudly into a cell phone.

# Chapter 28

We managed to get away somewhat scot-free, and I learned a very interesting fact. Belmont could've been a race-car driver in a previous life. I knew as a zombie, a car crash probably wouldn't kill me, but I still reached for the "oh-crap" handle when he yanked the wheel and made a turn going sixty miles an hour.

We heard sirens all over the roads. Of course there would be after the sheriff's wife had just been attacked. A guaranteed signal for the whole cavalry.

Belmont ditched the car in the Walmart parking lot, figuring the authorities had no real way to link him to it since he had paid for it with cash and hadn't registered it, and we went our separate ways with a plan to meet up the following afternoon.

That night, I slept wearing a ski mask. Scratch that. I laid down wearing a ski mask. No sense in taking risks anymore. I had no idea when I would be summoned again, but I knew it would be soon, especially if Carlson suspected us of staking out his house. If I got caught out in the open without cover, I would be busted. Probably with a baseball bat. The ski mask gave me just an ounce of security. It made it all the more difficult for someone to recognize me as I staggered through the streets searching for my next kill.

As I had feared, the summoning took place sometime after eleven. I felt the effects coming on. Not like before when I first went under—no, this was different. Over the course of the last few weeks, I must have evolved. This time, I knew the summoning had started before I went under the spell.

My eyes grew hazy. I experienced that strange tugging at my stomach. Like someone had tied a string on my belly button and was trying to pull me inside out. I didn't want to go. I wanted to resist in my mind, but my body acted on its own.

Soon, I left my house and entered the road. The journey to the cemetery lapsed in real time for me. I walked ten miles at a rapid pace and covered the distance in less than two hours. There were cars out, and they whizzed past, as did houses, stores, and eventually trees and forest. I entered the cemetery by climbing the rear fences.

When I arrived at the mausoleum, I descended the stone steps of the passageway, passing in front of the necromancer, unable to turn my head to stare at him, though I tried everything within my power to will myself to look. Now was my chance to confirm his identity. I felt his eyes boring into the back of my skull.

Belmont wasn't here. Was this where Sheriff Carlson punished me for breaking into his home and nearly killing his wife? Was this where he sent me to murder my own family? I couldn't focus in on this now, because the voice in my head dispelled all other thoughts.

I heard the necromancer laugh. It didn't sound mirthless or sinister, but he found something to be genuinely humorous. It took me only a moment to realize it.

My ski mask.

The fool thought it was hilarious. As he reached for my mask to remove it, that was where something went wrong.

I moved out of his way. Not by much. Just a shifting of my head away from his reaching hand. This action caused him to seethe with anger. His voice grew louder, chanting some devilish language, trying to break my will. I still comprehended my surroundings, but this new mantra prevented me from moving unless commanded. I knew he was in control, and he must've known it as well, but my defiance for one brief moment disturbed him enough that he didn't reach to remove my ski mask again.

How had I done it? The question lingered in my mind even as he gave me my new assignment. I didn't hear a name, but he placed something in my hands. A rag? No. A towel. Wet, but not with blood.

Sweat.

I wanted to drop the filthy object and wash my hands clean of it, but I was powerless to do anything but wring the fabric between my fingers. My senses heightened, and I knew inwardly where to go. I didn't know whom this towel belonged to, but they were in grave danger now.

Slinking through the woods toward my destination, I stuck close to the road, but never stepped out in the open. More than an hour had passed when I finally arrived. The house bore some familiarity to me, but I couldn't remember why. Still, I felt overjoyed when I saw that it was not my own home, and took strength in knowing my family would live at least another day.

Entering through the back porch, quiet and using a stealth I didn't usually possess in reality, I stepped through the living room. I passed through the kitchen and then began ascending the stairs. At the top, I headed directly for the back bedroom. As I entered, I saw them—both of them, a man and a woman—and my rage took over. I lost consciousness for what seemed like only a moment, but when my mind resurfaced, I stood over a body. The woman screamed at me, and I stared down at the victim.

It was Sheriff Carlson. His blood on my hands. His eyes closed. Not moving.

The sheriff was not the necromancer!

And now I had finally murdered. Belmont was nowhere to be seen. Just me. Guilty.

Then I noticed something vital. Sheriff Carlson was still alive. His chest rose and fell with his breathing. I saw blood trickling down from his left ear where I had struck, but I knew I wasn't finished yet. I had been commanded to kill him, and there was no way I could disobey.

In a state of hysteria, Mrs. Carlson screamed for help and begged for me to stop. She glared at my face through streaming tears, but there was no recognition because, thankfully, I was still wearing the ski mask.

I wasn't a killer! But it wasn't my choice. Or was it? I clung to those words.

*I am not a killer. I am not a killer.*

I repeated this until I felt the strength returning to my vocal cords.

"R . . ." I started to utter. Only one letter, but quite an accomplishment nonetheless. My feet forced me toward her to attack, but I hung on to those words once more. *I am not a killer.* It took all my strength and control to open my mouth.

"Rrr . . . uh . . . nnn," I slurred.

Nothing happened. Mrs. Carlson still cried, but she looked at me, confused.

Had I actually said the word, or had it just appeared in my head?

"Rrr . . . uh . . . nnn now!" I shouted at the top of my lungs. This time, I heard it with my ears, and so did Mrs. Carlson. She scrambled from the bed and I lunged for her, raking her nightgown with my hand, but she fell out of reach. I tried to stop myself again, to issue another warning, but all I was able to do was collapse on the bed and mumble into the pillow. I lay there only for a second and then rose up again. Time to finish off the sheriff. I turned to fall upon him and noticed Mrs. Carlson hadn't left yet. She had retreated to the closet, and stood bent over a pile of clothing.

Was she stupid or something? I gave her an opening—a chance to escape—and she was too dumb to take it.

Taking a deep breath, concentrating wholly on one thought once more—*I'm not a killer*—my words flowed freely from my lips.

"Leave now! I can't stop myself!" I shouted. "You've got to run away from me!"

"Why are you doing this?" the woman pleaded.

I took two steps toward the closet, trying to force out an answer.

Mrs. Carlson turned, holding a rifle.

The first shot rattled the windows, but missed me completely. I growled and dove toward her as the second shot struck me in the neck. I didn't feel any pain, but I could feel the bullet lodge in the hollow of my throat.

Mrs. Carlson started to sob. She obviously thought the nightmare was over, but she tripped backward when, instead of falling to my death, I took more steps toward her.

"I said run!" My voice gurgled like a bone in a blender.

I wondered if Belmont would be able to mend this injury.

Mrs. Carlson finally heeded my warning and bolted past me. I managed to yank the sleeve of her nightgown, but then she vanished from view and I started after her.

Down the stairs. Through the kitchen, the back door, out on the porch, and into the yard. She screamed madly, zigzagging across the neighbor's yard, where she pounded on the door with her fists. Lights snapped on in the windows. This was no longer a private party, but I couldn't stop myself. I stepped toward the neighbor's yard, but then finally managed to halt my progress.

"I am not a killer!" I growled out loud, and then my mind went blank.

Seconds passed, then a minute, then two. My eyes opened. I found I still stood in the yard, but now had control of my movement. The summoning had ended. I couldn't believe it. And then I saw Mrs. Carlson screaming and pointing in my direction. People dressed in night-clothes, pajamas, and robes filed out of the neighbors' house. One of them had a handgun.

The man took aim and fired. The bullet only grazed my cheek, but it definitely helped to get my wheels turning. I bolted for the woods beyond the backyard. More shots rang out. They missed, and I took cover in the trees. I looked behind me, but no one was following. Instead, I watched them race for the Carlson house to aid the fallen sheriff.

# Chapter 29

Belmont removed the bullet and placed it in my withered palm, then went to work on my damaged vocal cords.

"It's not Sheriff Carlson!" I gurgled.

"What a mess!" he said.

"But the chimes . . ."

"Either you imagined it, or the necromancer was nearby. Perhaps watching the sheriff," Belmont replied.

I watched his eyes as they concentrated on the surgery. He had tools. A scalpel, forceps, some sort of soldering iron, a needle and thread. I felt his fingers digging in my throat, stretching the flesh, and I noticed the wisps of gray smoke rising up from my singed skin, feeling relieved I couldn't smell it.

"It's not him," I repeated. "We were wrong."

"I heard you the first time," Belmont said. "Try not to talk. You're making it difficult for me to work."

An hour passed. It was almost five a.m. My dad would be waking up soon for work. He probably wouldn't check in on me, but if he did . . .

Belmont finished and handed me a mirror. The skin

around my Adam's apple looked stretched and sewn together. Fifteen tightly woven stitches formed a zipper up my throat. I took a breath, and though I heard the faintest wheezing sound deep within my lungs, my breathing felt normal. Belmont handed me a bandage and helped me apply it over the wound.

"Now. What happened?" he asked, collapsing back onto the mattress and staring expectantly at me. I told him everything, and included all the details, particularly the ones involving my full comprehension. I told him about how I defied the necromancer by not letting him remove my ski mask and how I was able to keep myself from killing the Carlsons. It took a while for Belmont to speak.

"You broke the summoning chain," he finally said. "I had heard that it is possible, but I've never been able to do it. Perhaps your will is much stronger than you know."

I stared in the mirror at the bandage on my neck, running my fingers over where the stitches were sewn, trying to think of some sort of injury to blame this on before my mom saw it.

"It wasn't that hard," I said. "I just had to focus on one thought over and over again, and somehow I was able to stop myself."

"What was your thought?" he asked.

"I am not a killer," I answered.

Belmont smiled. "Interesting."

"I think you could do it too, if you tried."

His smile wavered. "I don't think so. I don't have any memory at all of what happens. I black out instantly, and my eyes open to the horror of what I've done."

"But have you tried preparing yourself?"

"How?" He leaned forward with his chin in his hands and his elbows resting on his knees.

"You know it's coming, right? Probably tonight. I wore a ski mask because I knew it would happen. We don't have to be killers."

"I was turned by a necromancer. I act differently when I'm summoned," he said. "That's just the way it is."

"But what if you could lie in bed and focus on one idea?" I asked. "A memory. A phrase. Something to help keep your concentration."

Belmont sniffed and wiped his nose with the back of his hand. "It's a good idea. Maybe I'll try it tonight."

"You don't believe it will work, though, do you?"

He grimaced and swallowed. "No, I do not."

"You don't understand everything about our way," I said. "You may be the smartest person I know and you've studied about zombies for decades, but that doesn't mean . . ."

Belmont held up his hand. "We've got work to do, and we only have a little time until I need to get you home before your parents find you missing."

"Yeah, but we're back to square one," I said, picking up a stack of newspapers to start the search over.

"Not exactly." He handed me the same newspaper with the article that had revealed Sheriff Carlson's connection to Naomi Dansbury. "I found this out a few hours ago, and I had planned to tell you later."

I searched the photo for any signs of someone I knew, but there were only unknown faces, other than Carlson.

"Look at where they held the funeral services," Belmont instructed.

"Jefferson First Presbyterian Church," I read. "So?"

"That was Reverend S. Maxwell Grossier's church before I killed him."

"Are you telling me she was a member of his congregation?"

Belmont nodded. "Which means she has, even in her death, more answers on the matter than we do."

I stared at Naomi's picture and felt a sinking sensation in my chest. Why couldn't we have figured out how to break the summoning spell before the night we took her life? Why couldn't we have stopped her from dying?

"Calvin?" Belmont said. I looked up from the photo. "Do you understand what we need to do?"

I sighed. "Break into her house while her husband's away at work?"

***

Belmont walked with me back toward Canterbury Avenue. He called me a taxi and handed me some cash as I waited outside of the Didman Dollar.

"Do you think you can duck out of school early again today?" he asked as we waited for my ride.

I shrugged. "It's not too hard."

"Do your parents know about your absences?"

"I don't think so, but I'm sure my friends are beginning to question what I'm doing." Jaylen would wonder what was going on. Maybe I should tell him. Hunting necromancers was seriously putting a strain on my friendships.

"Then it's set. Naomi Dansbury lived on 440 East Ofelia Avenue in Jefferson. It will be easy enough to find, and we can stake out the house later this afternoon."

Putting a stop to the necromancer would help Belmont's life get back to normal as well. Unfortunately, I wasn't too eager about staking out the Dansbury household. Breaking and entering was the type of lifestyle that was destined to get someone, namely me, killed.

# Chapter 30

Later that morning, I pulled on a turtleneck, one from the back of the closet because no one in high school wore turtlenecks if they could help it, and a fresh pair of jeans. It wasn't the greatest idea, going to school, but I didn't want to be home so my mom would start asking questions. Downstairs at breakfast, like so many mornings before, I found her glued to the television.

An angry Sheriff Carlson glared at the camera and called out a threat to their attempted killer. The interview failed to feature his wife, but several of the neighbors described the perpetrator—short, skinny, wearing a ski mask.

I wasn't short! I mean, I never had a future in basketball, but there were hundreds of kids at school who had to look up to me. Still, they didn't have enough information yet, and so far, no suspects.

Jaylen sat next to me on the bus, a knowing look on his face.

"What did you do?" he demanded. "Was that you?"

My heart started to pound. I felt sick, but I couldn't

lie to him. I needed Jaylen on my side, and lies would break that trust to pieces. So I nodded.

"Sheriff Carlson?" His eyes widened. "Why would he want to kill him?"

At least Jaylen was still blaming this on the necromancer, which was a huge win for me.

"I don't know!" My voice rose with agitation. "But I managed to stop myself completely, and I broke the summoning spell."

"That's good, right?" Jaylen thumped me on the shoulder with his mitt. "So who's next?"

"How should I know?"

Jaylen pointed to the bandage on my neck. "Bullet hole?"

"Bullet hole," I answered.

"Oh, dang!" He covered his mouth, smiling. "Bro, let me see."

"Not here! Are you crazy?" I looked around the bus and then back at Jaylen. "It's nasty, though. I look like Frankenstein."

"Frankenstein's monster," Jaylen corrected. "And you will if we add some knobs to the side of your throat."

Instead of focusing on the task awaiting me later that night, I started to think about school. I was failing Geometry and English. We had a pop quiz in World History the other day and I scored a twenty-two percent. The only answers I got right were the ones I guessed on. I had typically been a B+ to A- student, but with all of my energies centered on our pursuit of the necromancer, I had zero time to study for school. Midterms were just around the corner. I was doomed.

"Hey," Jaylen said as the school bus roared up next to the school and everyone stood to exit. "My parents just installed a new security system in our house."

"Oh," I said. "That's awesome."

"Do you want to know what we picked as a security code?"

I scratched my chin. "I guess, sure."

Jaylen chuckled. "Fat chance, sucker. Like I'm really going to tell you how to break into my house." He laughed louder, and I knew it was his way of easing the tension with humor, but the joke still hurt.

"Come on, Jaylen, you know I'd never do that to you," I said half-heartedly.

Jaylen's smile weakened and his eyes grew slightly serious. "Like you'd have a choice."

***

Just after lunch, Belmont picked me up in a black station wagon and took me down to the alley across from the Cobalt.

"I made special arrangements with Samuel," he said, pointing to a corpse lying lifeless beneath a white sheet. "I don't think it's wise we go out hunting on an empty stomach anymore. It will make us more vulnerable to the sorcery."

He pulled back the sheet and I stared upon a thin woman, early forties, with curly red hair. I looked away from the body even though my stomach churned greedily.

"I don't think I can do this right now," I whispered.

Belmont gripped my shoulders. "You don't seem well. Is there something you want to talk about?"

"No," I lied. "I just don't want to eat her."

Belmont released his grip and an understanding formed in his eyes. "You're feeling guilty, and you think by forgoing eating and punishing yourself, you'll find some sort of peace."

"That's not it," I said, my words harsh. But that was exactly how I felt. He couldn't have picked a worse time to spring a surprise meal on me. It was just the thing to push me over the edge.

"You need to feed," Belmont said.

"Feed?" I shouted. "Feed! No, it's *I need to eat*. Feeding is the term used for animals, and we're not animals."

The room felt claustrophobic. I didn't want to be here anymore with Belmont. I wanted to be back in class, finishing my homework. I wanted to attend baseball practice after school and maybe call a girl and ask her out.

Belmont brushed past me and removed the hacksaw from underneath the gurney. I glanced up at the woman's closed eyelids and imagined her sleeping peacefully. Other than her pale and sunken skin, there weren't too many differences between her and some regular person taking a nap. I had grown tired of desecrating dead bodies. Tired of eating . . . feeding on brains. And then I thought about Naomi Dansbury. Her screaming, pleading words, begging for mercy, and I snapped.

"Don't do it!" I shouted. Belmont looked up just as he readied to make a cut. "I said I don't want to eat right now."

"Then when?" he asked in frustration. "Later tonight? Tomorrow? It doesn't matter, Calvin. You'll have to do it again, or you'll do much worse." The saw blade rested against her forehead, but I struck out and knocked it out of his hand.

"I'm different than you. Maybe I can fight the urges longer. What if I don't have to eat like this?"

Belmont faced me. He held his hands at his sides non-aggressively, but he wore a stern expression. "You're not that different. Yes, you've done things I can't imagine doing, and that gives me hope of maybe one day understancing why all of this had to happen, but you still need to eat in the same manner as the rest of us do. It's not a risk worth taking."

I stood defiant. "I think you're wrong."

Belmont reached out for me, but I slapped his hand away. "I understand you're angry and frustrated, but remember, I'm here trying to help you," he said. "I'm not your enemy. I don't have all the answers, but believe me, if you don't eat, you will hunt and kill for food. Think about your parents. Think about your friends."

"I'm not like you. I'm not going to kill my family. I can stop it. Maybe you could've stopped from killing your family, too, if you hadn't been so weak."

Belmont's hand struck me right across the mouth. I felt no pain from the blow, just shock. I stumbled back and lost my footing, and had to regain control of my balance by holding the dead woman's ankles. I looked at Belmont, enraged that he had hit me, but saw equal anger in his eyes. I knew if I said another insulting word about him and his family, he would strike again. As bad as I hated this man right now, I didn't have the energy to fight him.

Instead, I walked away.

# Chapter 31

I headed off in the direction toward home. My heart wasn't in it to go investigate another house. Maybe tomorrow I would feel differently. I passed cars and people riding bikes. After a while I passed buses. School had ended for the day. Jaylen would be heading home. That was where I should be, but I didn't want to go there now. My dad would be gone for the evening with work, but my mom might be there, and she would want to know about my day. I would have to lie to her again, and I was sick of doing that. I wanted to be alone, but I didn't want to be in my house. I turned and headed back the way I came.

Walking faster now, frustration still lingering within me, my thoughts blurred and scattered. I was angry, but not at Belmont anymore. Yeah, he was the one who had turned me into this monstrosity, but I had to forgive him for that and move on. It wasn't his fault. He had become a creature of instinct, no different than a lion striking its prey.

As the neon lights of the Cobalt flashed to life, I considered heading back into the alley to confront Belmont, but instead I entered the pub through the front doors and found all the seats and tables empty. A heavyset woman with short, cropped hair stood behind the bar, stocking the shelves with glasses.

"Can I help you?" Expecting something gruff and distrusting, I was surprised when the woman spoke in a soft, pleasant voice.

"I'm just . . ." I started, shaking my head, confused. "I don't know why I'm here."

"You're not here to sneak a drink, are you?" she joked.

I grinned. "Not me." I was sixteen and I looked sixteen, and sadly, I would look sixteen for the rest of my life. So much for fake IDs.

The bartender finished with the glasses and pushed a small tray of mixed nuts toward me across the countertop. "Help yourself to those. I have to go in the back. Don't come behind the counter, though, or I'll suspect you of mischief." She smiled again, but I could sense the gravity of her words. I should have known this woman if she lived in Jewkes, but I couldn't place her face.

Now alone, I moved to the bar and stared at the nuts. Cashews, peanuts, almonds. Despite her vigorous wipedown, the counter looked dirty and the bowl smudged with fingerprints, but the nuts looked amazing. I couldn't remember wanting so badly to eat peanuts before. They had never been my favorite, but staring at them made me think of forbidden fruit, covered in salt and other spices.

It brought up one of my last memories of eating nuts. It was during the Christmas holidays nearly a year ago. They were cinnamon-glazed almonds. My dad loved those, and of all the nuts I had eaten, they were my favorites. We would eat them while watching the evening news, and I would steal as many as I could from the bag until I felt sick.

It was a good memory.

I grabbed a handful from the bowl and held them up to my mouth.

*Don't do it,* I thought to myself. *You'll just throw them up.*

It was true. I would. I had done it with everything else I had eaten over the past two months, and I didn't expect there to be a different outcome. Yet I didn't care. I opened my mouth and shoved the handful in.

Nothing.

No flavor.

Just hard, cracked pieces of plastic, or brittle wood. It wasn't food to me anymore.

I munched the nuts, but instead of spitting out the wasted bits, I thought of the cinnamon-glazed almonds from a year ago and tasted them as I chewed. The memory came vivid and sharp. I grabbed another handful and then another. I ate and remembered until the bowl sat empty and I licked my fingers, imagining the taste of salt and cinnamon.

The woman returned and noticed the empty container. "Hungry, huh?" she asked, snatching the bowl and wiping it with a towel tucked in her apron.

"Not anymore," I said. "Thank you."

"Kids like you shouldn't hang out in bars," she grumbled, winking.

Kids like me.

And then it dawned on me. I could beat this. I could find a normal, happy medium. I could live my life between those two worlds and find balance. Yes, I was going to throw up the stupid nuts about thirty minutes from now, and yes, I was going to eat that dead woman's brain on Belmont's slab sometime today, but life wasn't over for me. Not by a long shot.

# Chapter 32

I couldn't find Belmont anywhere. He wasn't in the room. Nor in the alley. The dead woman still lay on the table, the sheet covering her body completely. Belmont hadn't eaten. I probably really pissed him off and I needed to apologize. I should have never said anything about his family.

I exited back into the alley and searched for his car. Missing as well. I had been gone for over two and a half hours. Belmont wouldn't go after me, especially after the argument we just had. I wondered if I should wait for him to return, but I had a gnawing sensation in my gut. If he wasn't there, he may have gone home to the meat-processing factory, but I didn't believe that either. Call it intuition if you wanted, but I knew where Belmont had headed. We had a game plan, and even though I had messed things up by freaking out earlier, it didn't change what we needed to do. Belmont probably didn't trust me anymore. He didn't believe I would be of any help to him in my current condition. Maybe he didn't want me to have to go through the same ordeal again, so he decided to go alone. It was a nice gesture, but incredibly idiotic.

Pulling out my wallet, I sifted through the bills. Twenty-seven dollars and some loose change. Lunch money I never needed to use. I didn't have a credit card, so I couldn't call an Uber, but maybe I had enough money for a normal taxi. Those things still had to exist, right?

It took about twenty minutes before the taxi showed up, and when the driver asked me where I needed to go, I didn't hesitate.

"To 440 East Ofelia Avenue in Jefferson," I said. "It should be easy to find."

# Chapter 33

The Dansbury residence seemed meager at best. A small rambler by a dead-end road next to a field with over-grown weeds—which provided good cover while I upchucked the nuts from the bar. A chain link fence with several sections toppled over or cut through formed a barrier around the outskirts of a front yard filled with tall, dead grass that hadn't been cut for months. It was almost December, but this was Louisiana. Until the ice storms hit, lawns still needed a good mowing.

The taxi turned around in the driveway and dropped me off. I doubted the driver knew who lived in that house, but he eyeballed me like some sort of criminal. Which I guess I kind of was.

There were three houses on the same side of the road as the Dansbury house. Two of them looked rundown and empty, but one had a couple of cars in the drive-way and a child's bike in the front yard. Ofelia Avenue couldn't even hold to lower middle-class. I spun around and searched for Belmont's car. I didn't remember notic-ing it when the taxi pulled up. The sun had lowered in the sky, and evening approached. I looked up at the house, and though it appeared empty, I couldn't be positive.

"Well, this was a bad idea," I muttered out loud. Where was Belmont? Had he gone in already, found what he was looking for, and took off? Was I too late to help?

He wouldn't have stayed here this long rummaging around. I had wasted all my money and had no way to get home, and I was almost twenty miles from my house. I thought about calling my parents to come pick me up, but that would raise too many questions. They would wonder why I had traveled so far away, and to the house of the recently deceased. I didn't want to deal with that.

"I'm such an idiot!" I shouted. I wanted to stomp something. Kick it and break it. Why had I been so rash and impulsive? If I would have stopped to think about this, I would have never come to this place. I could have easily waited for Belmont in his room. Now I would have to find my way back, with no way to make it home for hours.

My parents would wig out on me. I was so angry with myself, I spat on the ground. Zombie spit was just like normal human spit, except it had a little thicker consistency, and I dribbled drool all over my chin and the front of my shirt. Every second I spent fuming in the Dansburys' driveway was a second I wasted when I should have been walking home.

I stared down the road toward the end of the subdivision and figured cutting through the field would save me some time since it was in the direction of Jewkes. But as I crossed into the taller weeds, I saw Belmont's car smashed head-on into a tree. Two tracks of dirt and thrown weeds marked the path he had taken, and smoke rose from the hood. I ran toward the car, and though the keys were still in the ignition, I didn't find anyone sitting in the driver's seat.

If this was Belmont's attempt at subtly sneaking into the Dansburys' house, I could have come up with at least a dozen better ideas than that. I thought back to when I rode along with him after we escaped the Carlson fiasco. He drove fast and wild then, but had remained in control of the car. Something had to have happened to cause him to drive off the road. And why did he leave the keys in the ignition? I looked back at the Dansburys' house. Could Belmont still be inside?

Ringing in my ears. Sharp and piercing. The sound brought me to my knees.

I couldn't remember it sounding so shrill.

This could only mean one thing, but it shouldn't be possible. Belmont had told me that the loudest ringing only happened when both the necromancer and a zombie were near the Lich Stone. This spot was miles from the mausoleum. Was this some sort of new power?

I rose to my feet as the ringing continued. I could sense I was being watched. Observed from close by.

And then I felt the all-too-familiar tug in my stomach and my mind went dark.

# Chapter 34

I woke up standing in an unfamiliar room. The lights were out, and I was unable to move. I could feel the power here, holding me at bay. The ringing in my ears sounded stronger than earlier, as though I were standing right next to a raging fire alarm. It was continuous and sharp, and it penetrated me to my core.

But that wasn't all. I could feel my body stiffening and quivering, my muscles in a constant state of constriction. It was as though I were being constantly electrocuted. Like someone had plugged a live wire into my skull, and it hurt something awful.

Actual pain. The first sensations of such I had felt since my turning.

"Calvin," a voice whispered, cutting through the sound and jolting sensation, if only for a moment.

If my skin could've formed goose bumps, there would've been some all over me. It wasn't Belmont's voice or the voice of someone familiar, like my parents. This voice belonged to somebody else, and whoever it was, I knew without any doubt that he was in control.

The necromancer.

I attempted to answer, but I couldn't muster a sound. I had no ability, my mouth numb and worthless, my teeth cemented together like a vice.

"You've been bad." The voice came from nearby. "You're different, aren't you?" he probed. "Than the other?"

Why was he asking me questions if I was unable to answer? But maybe if I concentrated . . .

"I noticed this when I first sent you to the reverend. I thought perhaps I had not recited the summoning correctly. But then you broke through when I sent you to kill the sheriff and his wife. You showed defiance that the other does not. How did you do it?"

I found the thought that had helped me break the chain inside the Carlsons' home, and I exerted all my concentration on that one idea. *I am not a killer. I am not a killer. I am not a killer . . .*

"But you are," the voice said, reading my thoughts. "You're *my* killer."

The invasion of my mind enraged me, and I concentrated wholly on blocking him out. I wasn't even sure how to do this, but I chose to repeat the phrase over and over again. My lips quivered, and my breathing escaped in short, quick bursts.

"No . . . I . . . am not," I muttered. My voice was barely a whisper, but I knew the necromancer had heard it. Silence followed. Well, not total silence. The ringing in my ears still persisted. I could sense that my ability to speak troubled him. He wasn't expecting me to do this, and it changed everything in his thought process.

After an extremely long and painful pause, he said, "You can speak, but can you move?" His voice was quizzical, even curious. I was a rat in his observation lab, and he was testing to see what I could do.

Oh, how badly I wanted to show him and prove to him that I could indeed move as I pummeled the life from him with my fists. But despite my best efforts fighting against the overwhelming force holding me at bay, I couldn't even wiggle a finger.

Then the air filled with thick energy. The ringing continued, but I couldn't figure out why. Where was I exactly? A light clicked on near the ceiling. It was electric, controlled by a dimmer. As the light grew in strength, my vision returned, revealing my surroundings. Although it felt as though I stood in a cloud, hazy and unclear, I could see that I was in an unfinished basement. Wooden wall studs, two-by-fours stacked on the floor, pieces of gypsum board resting against a concrete foundation, copper piping. There was a desk in front of me, with a book opened in the middle to some illustration, and in the corner of the room, I saw something that explained everything to me.

The Lich Stone.

Somehow, the necromancer had moved it from its original location in the mausoleum to his home. I'd love to think it impossible, but my eyes didn't deceive me. The stone had to have weighed a ton and would have taken at least two people to move it, but it was there, and it felt much stronger. The symbols remained dormant, but I knew that could change at any moment. I also saw the outlines of an image drawn on the floor around me. A circle of chalk and the pointed ends of a star. I was standing inside a hand-drawn pentagram. I felt hopeless, but then I realized something even more disturbing.

Focusing all my concentration on that one thought again, I finally managed to move, turning my head just a few inches. The action caused the necromancer to gasp with delight as I saw Belmont standing beside me, entranced, frozen in place and under the necromancer's spell. Around him, the pointed corners of another pentagram stretched out in all directions. The necromancer had caught both of us. Belmont must have driven his car into the tree when the necromancer had summoned him.

Something grazed my shoulder. Fingers. Immediately, a cold sensation entered my body, icicles shooting through my veins as my heartbeat shot into overdrive. My eyes didn't move, but they didn't need to. The necromancer stepped out from behind me and crossed my path.

Hooded in the same dark burgundy robes from before, filthy and covered in thick, tarlike stains, the necromancer didn't stand more than an inch or two taller than me. A gossamer trail of smoke rose from his fingers, where he held a small stick of what looked like incense. It couldn't be incense, because I wasn't able to smell that. But I could smell this, and my thoughts immediately went to blood.

"Attack me if you desire it," the necromancer whispered.

This wasn't an actual command, otherwise I'd have no choice but to obey. It was a challenge. A taunt. A test to see the bounds of my abilities. I would love to attack him. To strangle him. Crack open his conniving skull and scoop out his brains. He must have known this too, but also knew he had control over me.

"Show me . . ." I started to stammer. "Show me . . . who . . . you . . . are." I wanted him to pull back the hood to see the face of the one we had been hunting all this time. I needed an image I could pinpoint my hate and blame on for all my misery. But he shook his head slowly.

"And ruin my fun?" He clicked his tongue behind his

teeth. "I don't think so." Then he laughed, and I found it more obnoxious than the ringing in my ears. "I knew you two would eventually come looking for me. It's no mystery. Naturally, when you discovered what you were and what you were doing in the wee hours of the morning, you'd want to know why. Your search would eventually lead you to me. So don't think I didn't know you'd appear one of these days, but I needed to continue my practice until I had grown strong enough to make more."

"Make more what?" My ability to speak had grown easier. I still had no control over my limbs, but the power preventing my speech was dwindling. I could sense it fading, and I no longer stammered as my words flowed freely.

"More of you, of course," he answered. "My own to use and not a couple of spares like you and the other. Mine will be more powerful and able to do terrible things. But you see, there are steps to take. It wasn't easy. In fact, it was very difficult. But the result will be so satisfying."

What was he talking about? I assumed he referred to his rise as a powerful necromancer, but I couldn't make sense of his arrogant babble.

"Now I no longer need your services," he said. "You'll be free of my control. That sounds good, doesn't it?"

It did sound good, but I knew there was a catch. If he no longer needed me, that meant he would kill me, because he knew I wouldn't stop until I caught him.

"But first I need to know how you broke the summoning chain. The other is much stronger, and from what I've determined, has been in this condition for a much longer time period than you, and yet he can't do the things you do. Why is that?"

The other? Why did he keep referring to Belmont as the other? It troubled me, but then I realized he had no way of knowing Belmont's identity. No public records of his life. Not since he murdered his family. The necromancer had no way of researching, and probably no means for hunting him down.

"It's not hard," I said. "You're not as powerful as you think you are. Maybe you need to read some more." I felt proud of myself for having the courage to fire an insult his way, but he only laughed.

"Oh, I'll continue to read and to study. And now that I have the stone in my possession, my powers will grow daily. Soon, I will move from this place and go somewhere else to dig deeper."

"Why?" I asked, certain his answer would be similar to that of any other psychopath that went on a murdering rampage.

"I don't need to answer that," he said.

"You've killed innocent—"

"No, he did that for me," the man interrupted, offering a slight head nod in Belmont's direction.

"It wasn't his fault. He had no control." I didn't know why I argued with him, but I wanted to force him to understand.

"Tell me, Calvin, how did you do it? How do you speak when no one else can? How did you move when I tried to touch you? How did you stop yourself from carrying out my orders and breaking the summoning chain?"

My eyes moved ever so slowly downward. I scanned his person, taking note of his small stature and frame. I was only sixteen years old, but if I weren't under his control, I could've taken him easily. His fingers holding the smoking stick were thin and bony, and then I noticed the golden glint of a ring on his finger. A wedding band. I didn't know why, but it shocked me. How could someone with a family turn so dark?

"There's no sense in keeping secrets. Come now," he coaxed.

"Show me who you are and I'll tell you everything."

The necromancer's hooded head cocked slightly to the left. I couldn't see his face, but I knew he was smiling. After a moment's pause, he said, "Very well." He raised his hands and removed the hood.

That face.

I knew it.

Where had I seen him before? He wasn't someone I had met personally, but someone I had seen only recently. The stranger waited patiently for me to piece it all together.

"Mr. Dansbury?" I said, as the recognition finally hit me.

"It's a pleasure to meet you," he answered.

Garrett Dansbury was the necromancer? But I had seen him on the news. He was crying, sobbing for his loss. He sent me and Belmont to kill his own wife!

"But Naomi?"

For only a moment, Garrett Dansbury's eyes twitched, but then his features hardened. "I didn't want to harm her, but she left me with no other choice."

"No other choice? She was your wife!" How could he have killed her? She was beautiful. Even if it wasn't with his own hands, he ordered her death.

"And she discovered what I had been doing. If she had just trusted me and left things alone, I wouldn't have needed to do what I did. The others did not need to die either."

"What others?" I asked.

"She went to our reverend first. He asked too many questions, and I couldn't let him leak the word out."

It all began to make perfect sense. "Then when you

killed him, she went to somebody else. The minister from another church."

He nodded. "I learned about their intended meeting in the park, and I had Colby killed. It was unfortunate. And since I could no longer trust her, Belmont took care of Naomi for me."

"And the sheriff?" I asked.

Mr. Dansbury grinned. "I was his prime suspect. I thought about giving you one more chance to prove your worth, but now I see you can't be trusted."

I felt the hold on my body weakening, and could almost move my neck to try and spot the best exit. I knew we were downstairs in the house, and if I could somehow break free, I should have no problem escaping.

"What are you going to do now?" I asked.

"A deal's a deal," Garrett said. "I kept my end of the bargain. Now tell me what it is you do that makes you different."

I stared at him, disgusted. "I'm not different."

"Yes, you are. I need to know why you have a weakening effect on my powers." He watched me, his eyes determined, wanting an answer. For him, to not know would be taking a risk. He had already done dark and terrible things. The next step would take him further into darkness.

Still, I kept quiet, making no attempt to answer.

"You're not going to tell me?" he asked.

I shook my head in defiance.

Garrett stared at his fingers and held the stick of blood closer to his face. "You're not going to break your promise, are you?"

"Get that thing out of my face!"

The necromancer sighed. "Very well. So long, Calvin

Simmons." Licking his fingers, he extinguished the burning ember in a cup of watered-down scotch.

At first, I didn't understand what this action accomplished, but then I heard an unnatural moan from somewhere behind me. Footsteps drew near. I could barely move, but managed to turn in time to see someone approaching, his eyes white and lifeless, his mouth gaping open lustfully. He still wore the Werner High hooded sweatshirt. I couldn't think of any explanation.

Why was Jaylen here? Why was he under the power of the necromancer? How could this have happened? But I had no time to think and piece together the puzzle as Jaylen surged toward me.

I tried to shout, but he fell upon me, pushing me down to my knees. As I pleaded for my life, I felt him sink his teeth into the flesh beneath the base of my skull.

# Chapter 35

Jaylen started biting my neck—he was going to feed on me. I felt no pain, only urgency. I had to stop him, even if it didn't make any sense. But as bite after bite of my flesh tore from the back of my neck, I felt hope vanishing.

I expected blood to gush from my neck and down my shoulders. But nothing came. Even if he got to my brain, he'd be disappointed. But then a sickening realization hit me: He didn't want to feed. He wanted to kill.

My fingers wiggled. They were stiff and the action proved difficult, but they formed a fist and I struck, hitting Jaylen in his forehead. My best friend made no reaction to my punch, but only continued moaning and biting.

Then I felt movement in my legs. I squirmed and managed to break free of his grasp as Mr. Dansbury watched our struggle. His eyes were bright and excited, and it occurred to me that he was watching a murder up close for the first time. The necromancer didn't speak, but moved out of our way as I tried to escape with Jaylen in pursuit.

"Jaylen! Focus in on my voice! Look at me!" I

demanded, but he had no recognition. No life in those cold, white eyes. I snapped my head toward Belmont, still standing stiff and lifeless in his own pentagram. "Belmont? Can you hear me?" This caused the necromancer to squeal with glee.

"Oh yes. Call to them. Help them break my trance. I really want you to," he said.

Jaylen's fingers curled downward like claws, and he lashed at me, ripping my shirt at the collar. Scrambling backward, I flailed my arms and snapped my fingers in front of me in a vain attempt to create a response. Like lightning, Jaylen's hand lashed out, snagging hold of my wrist with amazing strength. The bone snapped, my hand dangling lifeless, flapping around in his grasp like a rag doll.

The sight of my severely injured limb ignited within me the reality of my impending death. Jaylen couldn't be stopped. Somehow, the necromancer had taken control over him. Had turned him. He must've learned of his friendship with me.

This was all my fault.

Yanking my arm to free myself from Jaylen's grip, I struck out once again with my other hand. The punch landed squarely below his chin, and for the first time, he stumbled backward. His grip around my wrist loosened and I swung again, this time landing a blow to the side of his head near the temple. He fell down to one knee.

Jaylen growled, but he didn't stop. As I readied myself to throw more punches and pound him into submission, I knew it wouldn't be enough. All I was doing was slowing him down. In order to end the fight, I would have to go after the necromancer.

I turned toward Garrett Dansbury and lunged for him—falling short as Belmont's arms closed around my legs by the knees. I toppled forward and felt his fingers work their way up my back. Dansbury was using both my friends to kill me. Flipping over, I warded off Belmont's attack with my legs, kicking out as hard as I could. One of my feet connected with his nose dead on, shattering something in his face. Cartilage or bone, or both.

All three of us were on our feet again. I swung with my broken wrist, but my hand flapped like a puppet, slapping Belmont with little effect. He wasn't interested in squaring off with me. With his arms outstretched and his fingers still curled like claws, he pounced. This time I reacted quicker, shifting to the side, and Belmont collapsed on Dansbury. It was a momentary victory, and I thought Belmont would begin attacking his master out of confusion, but instead Belmont screamed in agony.

Jaylen froze as we watched the horror in silence. I had never heard Belmont make such an awful sound, as though he were suffering the worst pain imaginable. Zombies were normally immune to pain, but Belmont could feel whatever was happening. He writhed on the ground, legs kicking, body trembling. As he rolled over, smoke rose up from where his clothing had been burned away and the flesh beneath seared, his skin red and bubbling. Pure pain and maybe even hatred formed in Belmont's eyes as he fell away from Dansbury, crumpling in an agonized heap on the floor.

The necromancer seethed. "Do you trust your defiance will save you from that pain?" He pointed to Belmont, still curled in the fetal position at his feet.

I looked at Belmont and then back at Dansbury. We couldn't touch him. A stronger power was at work there, and I would suffer a similar fate as Belmont if I attempted to go after the necromancer.

"I am still your master," Dansbury whispered.

Jaylen fell on me again, his nails jabbing into my shoulder and hooking beneath the skin. I pulled forward, braced my leg against the corner of the table, and spun around, swinging my good hand as hard as I could. The blow nailed Jaylen in his left eye, and he staggered away.

I had to get out of here, but as I moved past Jaylen and reached for the unfinished handrail of the stairs, Mr. Dansbury took a step toward the Lich Stone, and the ringing in my ears magnified in strength.

"If you run away, Calvin, I will make this last longer. I will draw it out for the two of you. Because we both know, he won't stop until he's fulfilled his summoning."

I made it to the first step, but hesitated, thinking about his words. It seemed pointless to run or hide. Belmont and Jaylen would find me. The summoning power was too great and the necromancer too powerful. I didn't want to bring this fight into my home, because I knew they would kill everyone in their path to get to me, including my family. In order to stop Dansbury, I would have to kill Belmont and my best friend. I didn't want to do it, but what choice did I have?

Stepping down, I picked up one of the loose two-by-fours and tightened my fingers around it as best as I could manage. Splinters entered my palm as Belmont rose to his feet, smoke still clinging around his burned skin.

"How did you do it?" I asked as Jaylen growled and stepped toward me. "How did you turn Jaylen into one of us?"

Dansbury chuckled. "Don't pin your handiwork on me."

"My handiwork?" I dodged Jaylen's swinging hand and pushed back with the end of the board.

"I met your friend this afternoon. I told him I knew

about you and what you had done," he said. "Jaylen wanted to help, so he agreed to answer some questions."

What was he talking about? "I didn't turn him into a zombie," I snapped.

"Oh, but you did. You see, when your fingernails scratched him during your altercation, the infection entered his bloodstream."

"He's never showed signs before now!" Jaylen looked like a true monster, eyes wild and teeth bared like an animal. I didn't know if I had it in me to do this. Sure, he didn't know me anymore. To him, I was only a target. But he was still my best friend!

"The infection doesn't always take root right away. Sometimes it's instant. Sometimes it takes weeks. Maybe even years. But it always takes root," Dansbury said, his voice like a purr. "When I learned of your little encounter and how there was a possibility of his turning, I took action. Now he's mine. Fully mine. You and the other could never fully be called my own creations. But Jaylen . . . he's so different."

Jaylen lunged for me, and left without any choice, I dropped my best friend with a vicious crack to the skull. I had never been one who could hit for power, and being one-handed put me at a severe disadvantage. Heck, I surprised myself at how powerful the hit had been. It didn't kill Jaylen, but even as a zombie, the blow registered enough disorientation to keep him down, fully incapacitated.

A moment passed where there was only silence. My eyes trained in on Belmont as he stood and reared back like a bull ready to charge. With one last plea, I called to him, hoping to register something in his mind.

"Belmont, you are not a killer," I said.

He charged and I swung with all my strength.

The board broke, splintering into several pieces against his skull, and another sound followed. A sickening snap of bone. Belmont's head bobbled to the side as he dropped limply to his knees, his neck broken.

Vibration reverberated up my good wrist, and now I was pretty sure I had two bad wrists, though neither hurt. But it'd been my only option.

All I could think about was begging for my friend's forgiveness and how, if possible, I'd mend this injury. But Belmont had his whole life to master this practice, and I had no idea how to repair a broken neck.

The necromancer applauded. I looked up at him and glared. This had all been very entertaining for him to watch because he knew of his safety. I couldn't attack him. Not unless I wanted to end up with burned skin or worse. Maybe I could have attacked had we been somewhere else. Somewhere farther away from the Lich Stone, but not here. Not in his den of evil.

I was doomed to suffer at the hands of this monster. He would continue to send Belmont and Jaylen until they finished the job. Then what happened next? More murders? I had no doubt. Just as Belmont had explained, the necromancer had tasted this power and craved more. He would never stop.

My mind raced as I tried feebly to search for a solution. I bent down next to Belmont and pressed one of the broken pieces of the shattered two-by-four under his chin. I could see no other way out of this. I had to end it now. First Belmont, and then Jaylen.

But how could I sever his head or smash his brain? I knew him. He was my friend and he wasn't himself. I knew killing them wouldn't end the ultimate problem, because as long as air filled the necromancer's lungs, he would continue to haunt me. Others would come next.

Maybe I wouldn't know them, maybe I would. If Dansbury had indeed grown strong in his powers, able to turn Jaylen in just a couple of hours, he would know how to turn others into zombies. There would never be peace in my life. Maybe I shouldn't fight anymore. I could let Belmont finish me off. I doubted there'd be much pain, if any. Perhaps there would be a chance for my family to be safe.

I lowered my weapon. It would be easier this way, and I would welcome death. To close my eyes and never again be forced to open them.

Belmont stirred. Jaylen moaned and I looked back at his prostrated body. Poor dude. He wasn't moving too well. As I closed my eyes, I felt Belmont's fingers fumbling on my chest. But it was not an aggressive action. I expected his teeth to tear into my skull at any moment, but instead I heard his voice as he spoke softly.

"I am not a killer," he whispered, where only I could hear.

I looked down at him and found recognition there for the first time since waking up in Dansbury's basement. Belmont's lips quivered as he smiled, and then I noticed his hand, and more importantly, what he held inside of it.

A grenade.

The backup plan.

He told me he only brought it with him when he believed there could be no other chance, which meant he had never intended to walk away from this.

"Belmont, no!" I whispered, as another sensation swarmed in my insides. An inward pull. Dansbury stood next to the Lich Stone, attempting to summon me once again.

"You see, Calvin," the necromancer uttered from somewhere close behind me. "Although you're an oddity, even you cannot withstand forever." The ringing rose to a deafening level in my ears, and my mind started going blank.

Belmont stood, his neck set at an odd angle, still holding on to the grenade.

"I miss my family," he muttered. "And I am so tired."

And then he pulled the pin.

Time slowed down, but even then, I knew this was headed for disaster. I had seen movies, and if they bore any accuracy, we only had a few seconds. I reached for Belmont, but he withdrew, backing toward his master.

"All you're doing is prolonging your death," Dansbury snarled. He couldn't see the grenade yet, and he had no idea what was about to happen.

Belmont gave me one last glance, mouthed the word "run," then he collapsed into Dansbury.

Bending down, I yanked Jaylen up under his armpits and held him in the crooks of my elbows. He fought me all the way, but I discovered a new level of strength and dragged him along as I bounded up the stairs. Belmont screamed in agony, the sound of his burning skin sizzling all around me, in my ears, in my head. I wanted desperately to plug my ears and drown out the sound of his cries of anguish.

"I'm so sorry, Belmont!" I shouted, seizing the doorknob at the top of the stairs and heaving Jaylen through the opening.

And then an explosion ripped through my world and the ringing finally stopped.

# Chapter 36

Parts of the main level collapsed inward, showering floorboards, carpet, and furniture down below. Debris landed everywhere. Somehow, I had survived. After performing a cursory check of my body, I discovered only the injuries Jaylen and Belmont had inflicted during our battle.

"Oh, my freaking head!" Jaylen groaned, no longer fighting me.

"Are you hurt?" I asked.

Jaylen rubbed his face, checking for wounds, but then whimpered. "I'm just dizzy. Shouldn't I be hurt?"

I felt sick for a second. Poor Jaylen had no clue what was going on. Now, the necromancer had thrust him headfirst into my world. How would he cope? How could I help him? I shook the thoughts away.

"You'll get used to it," was all I managed to say.

It was a miracle we had managed to stay up above, since the blast from the grenade tore a gaping hole right through the living room floor. We could see all the way down. So much dust swirling. A fire blazed, and most of the wooden studs burned a brilliant orange in color. Thick smoke billowed as everything ignited.

No coughing. No sounds.

Mr. Dansbury was dead.

I didn't need to search the rubble to confirm it. His hold on me and Jaylen through the Lich Stone had been cut off like a severed limb, and I knew he was no more.

But that meant Belmont was gone as well.

"Where are we?" Jaylen asked, looking around.

"Garrett Dansbury's house."

"Who?" He looked utterly confused.

"There's no time to explain it. There's going to be people coming to find out what happened. They'll be here soon. Ambulances. Firemen. Police officers. We have to go!"

Jaylen considered this instruction and then nodded. "Right. Let's bounce."

But I didn't want to leave Belmont like that. Not in that state. Not out in the open for the world to see. What would they say when they found him? He hadn't existed for over a hundred years.

Closing my eyes, I thought of my friend one last time. I didn't think of him helping me adapt to being a zombie. I didn't think of him eating. I thought of him sleeping next to his wife and his two daughters. Finding peace and able to rest. The empty casket finally filled.

# Chapter 37

Samuel sat on a rusted metal folding chair. In the next room, behind the locked door, business in the comic book shop went on as usual, with the owners unaware the three of us were sitting here. It had been two days since the death of the necromancer and my friend Belmont, and outside in the alley, the Cobalt was about to open.

He wasn't what I expected.

Samuel.

Belmont's creepy delivery guy.

I always imagined him greasy. Slick black hair with way too much mousse. A week's worth of stubble. Chomping on a toothpick. Probably wearing eyeliner and possessing a foul mouth.

But I was wrong.

The man sitting in front of Jaylen and me bore an image on the other end of the spectrum.

He stood taller than us, but not quite six feet. Medium build, with light blond hair and blue eyes. He wore a class ring on his finger and a calculator watch on his wrist. Chewing on gum, with his hands wedged in the pockets of a ski parka and a backpack crammed with college text-books resting on the floor next to his leg.

"Who are you guys, exactly?" he asked, chomping nervously and sizing us both up.

"It's not important," I answered.

"Yeah, well, I don't know what you're talking about," Samuel said.

"Yes, you do," Jaylen replied.

I found Samuel's telephone number in a manual yesterday at Belmont's place. No one knew about his small apartment hidden within the abandoned meat-processing factory, which gave me free rein to search the place in privacy. Samuel answered when I called and almost hung up on me. That was until I mentioned I knew all about his extremely illegal activities. After that, he showed up to our meeting, right on time.

Samuel's left knee bobbed up and down like the wings of a hummingbird, but we kept our cool. It was extremely important that we did. Everything depended on how this exchange played out.

"So what are you going to do?" Samuel asked. "Turn me in? Call the police? I have an alibi. I can beat it."

I licked my lips and leaned forward. "We're not going to turn you in."

Samuel's knee stopped bobbing and his eyes narrowed. "You're just messing with me. What do you want?"

"We need your help."

I had grown up a lot over the past two days. I missed Belmont and felt so much guilt for what had happened to him. When the dust settled at the Dansbury residence, it raised a ton of questions. No one knew what to make of the mess. When asked, the neighbors were of no help. Garrett Dansbury had always been reclusive and strange.

His wife, Naomi, had always done most of the talking. When she died tragically, Garrett became even more of a recluse and had rarely been seen.

But what of the weird items in his house? Yes, there was that stone . . . odd, but not really of importance. What drew most of the investigators' attention were the items found hidden in a suitcase in Garrett's bedroom. Items they managed to save once they took control of the fire. After DNA testing, the towel covered in the dry sweat of Sheriff Carlson and the lock of Naomi's long black hair didn't raise too many eyebrows. The shirt covered in Reverend S. Maxwell Grossier's blood from a car accident that happened just prior to his murder and the severed finger of George Oldman, the transient murdered mysteriously under the Jefferson Bridge, did however. Oddly, police investigators found objects from each of the murdered victims in Garrett's suitcase.

Then, although they already had enough evidence to confirm their suspicions that Garrett had indeed been the murderer, searching the rubble in the basement revealed something else strange. They found body parts, but not just Garrett's. After extensive research, they concluded Garrett must have been somewhat of a grave robber, because the other parts they found belonged to a body that had been dead for quite some time.

Vindicated? Yeah, I definitely thought so. But now life had to continue on for me and, unfortunately, for Jaylen as well.

And Jaylen had yet to eat his first meal.

I could see the frustration brewing in his eyes. The hunger. The rage threatening to kick in. Unless we tied up this one loose end with this Samuel guy, we could be in some trouble.

"My help?" Samuel asked. "How so? And where exactly has Belmont gone again?"

"He went back home to his old job, but he left me here to continue his work on neurobiology," I said, trying my best to sound educated.

"Give me a break, kid." Samuel slumped, palming his face and wiping at his eyes. "I'm not an idiot."

"He's telling the truth," Jaylen said.

"And who are you?" Samuel asked.

Jaylen scoffed. "I'm his business associate, fool. What do you think?"

"You two don't even know what neurobiology is." Samuel looked toward the door and reached for his backpack.

"Of course I do," I said. "My particular interest is in the cognitive results of direct stimulation in brain synapses specific in postmortem subjects. Or, as you know, in the brains of the recently deceased." What a mouthful! It took me two hours to put that little phrase to memory after reading all about it at Belmont's place.

Samuel hesitated. His hand closed around the leather strap of his pack, but he didn't pick it up off the ground. I must have impressed him.

"What are you, some kind of kid geniuses?" he asked.

I feigned innocence and shrugged. "We don't like to refer to ourselves as such, but yes, I suppose we are."

"And Belmont wants you to continue his research by yourself?" Samuel asked, scrunching his nose in confusion.

I couldn't tell if he was buying this or not. His eyes looked strained, as though trying to process all this information.

"Not exactly by ourselves. Belmont will be checking

in on us from time to time to review our research. But for
the most part, yes, we'll be doing this by ourselves."

Samuel gnawed on the inside of his cheek. "Suppose
I say no?"

"Bad move, dude!" Jaylen blurted out. "Then we go
to the police and tell them everything you've done." It
was mean, but we had to be mean in order to survive.

"They'll arrest you too!" Samuel glared at Jaylen and
then at me. He didn't like us at all. Honestly, I thought he
was trash myself, but you did what you had to do.

"We're just minors," I said. "We'll play it innocent,
and they won't do a thing. And Belmont is long gone.
I don't even know where he's at, to tell you the truth.
And what are you going to say? A mysterious man named
Belmont paid you to do it? Come on. You don't really
believe the police will buy that, do you?"

Samuel scoffed. I had no doubt he wanted to smack
us right in our faces, but we had him where it hurt and
he knew it.

"It's like I don't have much of a choice," he grunted.
"I don't like it."

"What's not to like?" Jaylen asked. "You'll still be
paid. In fact, Belmont has agreed to give you a raise."

This piqued his interest. "How much?"

I looked at Jaylen for a moment, unsure of why he
had said that. I had no idea how much Belmont paid
Samuel, but I knew it was a lot of money. It would have
to be for Samuel to perform this shady service.

"Ten percent," I said, curling my lip.

Samuel slouched even lower in his chair and closed
his eyes. His lips moved as he counted. "So three hundred
and thirty dollars a delivery?" he asked.

I almost breathed a sigh of relief. Here I thought Belmont had paid him thousands. Still, three hundred and

thirty dollars every three days added up quickly. Luckily, I knew where Belmont stashed his cash. And there were bucket loads.

"And all I have to do is deliver the bodies here like before?" Samuel added.

"And no one can know about this," Jaylen said. "No questions."

Samuel smirked. "It's not like I want people associating me with you weirdos."

I rolled my eyes. Yep, I could do it now. And if that wasn't enough to make me want to do backflips, I actually performed my own embalming on myself last night. It only took me five hours. Jaylen helped and we made a disgusting mess, but I had never felt fresher. We also found some old textbooks and fixed my arms with steel plates, short wood screws, and some epoxy for my skin. I finally had a normal neck again.

"So you'll do it?" I asked.

Samuel rose and strapped on his backpack. He shrugged and walked to the door.

"Wait!" I said, raising my voice. "Are you going to do it or not?"

"Sure, man. I'll do it." Then he walked out.

Relief. We could relax now. After everything we'd been through, this little meeting with Samuel almost caused me to break out in a sweat.

Almost.

Life could return, finally, to normal.

# Chapter 38

"So what did it taste like?" Jaylen asked. His feet were propped up on the dash, and he had lowered the passenger seat practically all the way down. I had just picked him up from his house and we were headed to the movies, driving in my mom's Suburban.

I frowned. "What did it taste like?" Admittedly, that wasn't the question I expected him to ask. Glancing sideways at Jaylen, I raised an eyebrow.

"Yeah, man! You can't just tell me something like that and not give me all the details." He slugged me in my arm and the Suburban swerved a little. Same ole Jaylen. Well . . . with some major variations.

"You really want to know what it tasted like?" I couldn't believe him.

Jaylen made an expression with his face, as if to ask who wouldn't want to know.

"Well, I guess it was awesome!" I exclaimed.

I felt good. Life was good. It had been three months since the death of Garrett Dansbury. I had a few hiccups along the way, but nothing too serious, and now things were officially back to normal. Like clockwork, Samuel made his deliveries almost every three days. Natural deaths were on the rise in Jefferson, which was good news for me and Jaylen. Mainly because we stayed fed and I was no longer blamed for the deaths. I had been reading a lot of Belmont's books lately to stay in the know on our condition. So far, I hadn't come up with a single cure, but I did find a few work-arounds, and I remained hopeful.

It was out there. Somewhere. And we were going to find it.

My grades had gone up. Not quite As, but close enough. My relationship with my parents had grown. I knew that went against one of Belmont's primary rules, but I figured I had a few years before I had to break off ties. I was only sixteen years old. I had time, even as a zombie. Until then, I'd just have to mesh and fit in. I still had Jaylen, and the two of us were thick as thieves.

"Was it as greasy as I remember?" he asked.

I smiled and winked.

I'd finally learned to keep down a piece of pizza.

# THE END

As a kid, Tyler H. Jolley always had a knack for storytelling. When he grew bored of old fables, he created his own exciting and unique worlds. Many years later, he still had so many new ideas and stories swirling in his head, but with nowhere to share them. That's when he put his pencil to paper and let the creative juices flow.

His breakthrough novel, EXTRACTED, came out in 2013 and swiftly became an Amazon Best Seller and Spencer Hill Press Best Seller. Since then, Tyler has been busy publishing over a dozen books.

He reexamined the publishing process and created an efficient way to get his countless ideas into print. Tyler definitely didn't like to work alone, so he restructured his writing methods into a team approach.

When he's not writing, you can find him at his orthodontic practice, mountain biking, or on the hunt for the perfect doughnut.

**Twitter:** @Docjolley
**Facebook:** https://www.facebook.com/tyler.jolley.319/
**Instagram:** https://www.instagram.com/tylerhjolley/

www.ingramcontent.com/pod-product-compliance
Lightning Source LLC
Chambersburg PA
CBHW030350200726
48286CB00013B/701